TALES FROM THE EDGE OF FOREVER

An Extraordinary Collection of Short Stories

First Edition

Published by The Nazca Plains Corporation
Las Vegas, Nevada
2010

ISBN: 978-1-61098-171-2
Ebook: 978-1-61098-172-9

Published by

The Nazca Plains Corporation ®
4640 Paradise Rd, Suite 141
Las Vegas NV 89109-8000

PUBLISHER'S NOTE

Tales from the Edge of Forever is a work of fiction created wholly by *Alexander Hammond*'s imagination. All characters are fictional and any resemblance to any persons living or deceased is purely by accident. No portion of this book reflects any real person or events.

Galaxy Photo, Sergii Tsololo
Mountain Photo, Yurok Aleksandrovi
Male Photo, Helder Almeida

Art Director, Blake Stephens

DEDICATIONS IN ALPHABETICAL ORDER

Thanks to some very special people...

Brian, for his 25th century tech support and laconic grin

Carolina, whose intelligence and uniquely indomitable spirit continually inspires and challenges

Elita, whose generous and totally unselfish nature helped me find my feet again

Jill, who'll never read this but who gifted me my love of reading (Thanks Mum)

Jordan, my dear friend, an outstanding writer and movie buff par excellence

Julian B, the very best friend one could ever ask for and the finest man I know

Julian P, the ever cheerful 'man from the movies'. Stay frosty Dude!

Lena, who despite being Swedish continually offers warmth and encouragement

Laura, whose gentleness, perceptiveness and dark humour always passes muster

Michele, for critiquing me relentlessly and affectionately since our schooldays…and whose support is never less than 110%

Pam, for her undying effervescent enthusiasm, great sleeve notes and cheeky smile

Philippe, who notwithstanding he's a bloody Frenchman always believed in me. Merci!

Jan Arzooman, my brutal and no nonsense editor!

Sheraz, test reader, valued friend and SF fan par excellence

TALES FROM THE EDGE OF FOREVER

An Extraordinary Collection of Short Stories

First Edition

Alexander Hammond

CONTENTS

CONTENTS CONTINUED...

THE END OF THE WORLD

The night was warm though not unbearably so. It was for nights like these that the lone figure walking along the beach had travelled so far. A balmy ambiance pervaded and with the sun long gone, the walker was content to note that the sand still held some of the Caribbean sun's fierce heat.

A full moon was high in the sky casting an unreal light across the beach. In the sea phosphorescence could be seen glistening enticingly just beyond the shore. The decision to walk back to the hotel was surely a good one. The baked fish at the restaurant had been more than satisfactory and the wine passable. Maybe the second brandy hadn't been such a good idea but after all, it was a vacation.

A shooting star flashed past overhead. The walker made a fervent wish with the merest hint of sadness. Amanda, with her stunning African features, was beyond reach as apparently were all women that the walker truly desired and that was that. One day, Sam thought ruefully, maybe tolerance would emerge and prejudice vanish. Perhaps I should have wished for that instead the walker mused. This reverie was interrupted by the flash of someone ahead lighting a cigarette.

The smoker was clearly visible in the moonlight. A woman in an adventurous bikini sat cross-legged, staring out to sea. She seemed to sense she was not alone and looked round. "Hi Sam," she said. Startled, Sam walked over to her. When the two strangers were only a meter apart the girl held up her hand and breathed, "Don't ask; just enjoy the view."

Sam made to speak again when the girl put her finger to her lips and patted the sand next to her. Rather awkwardly Sam sat and stared out to sea. After a few seconds the urge to speak was almost unbearable. As if sensing this the girl said, "Silence is a deep well in which all things can be found. You must reach into it and take that which you need."

It appeared that this was both a conversation opener and closer at the same time. Evidently enjoying Sam's awkwardness she said brightly, "I'm here to watch the end of the world."

"Tonight?" Sam offered.

"Most definitely," the girl confirmed.

As the girl looked round to venture these comments her face was fully disclosed in the light of the full moon. She was beautiful. There was something Oriental about her but there was so much else in the mix. Her hair was long, black and straight and reached to her waist. She had unusually wide almond shaped eyes. Her exquisitely shaped cheekbones accentuated finely defined features that were as sublime as Sam had ever seen. Her skin was flawless and the dramatic curves of her physique completed the perfect picture.

"Aren't you afraid?" Sam asked.

"Of what?" the girl replied.

"The end of the world?"

"Of course not," she replied, with a light laugh.

Beguiled, Sam pressed on. "Why have you chosen to watch it from here?"

"Because here is where it's going to happen," was the enigmatic reply.

They both stared out at the sea in silence for several minutes before Sam plucked up the courage to speak again.

"What makes you think that the world is going to end?"

The girl laughed. "For something to begin something has to end. It's the truth of all things. Summer must end for autumn to begin. A flower must die to produce seeds for a new plant. Beginnings are endings. Endings are beginnings."

The brandy and this stranger's beauty were having a profound effect. Desperately trying to keep up with the eclectic thought process Sam continued, "So if this world ends, what's going to come after it?"

The girl stared back and murmured so quietly it was almost impossible to hear, "It is not of this world I am speaking."

Sam could smell her perfume now, heady, musky. She seemed to be everywhere.

"This is the moment that your world ends," the girl almost whispered, "And your new one begins."

As they embraced Sam felt as never before. The deliciousness of the girl's femininity descended like a blissful mist as her long nailed fingers began their sensual exploration. Within moments the girl skilfully liberated Sam's skirt from her tanned legs and started on the buttons of her flimsy blouse.

- The End -

ARTISTIC LICENCE

Being an immortal pan dimensional being, the entity didn't understand his creativity knew no boundaries; indeed he wouldn't have understood the concept of limitation even if you'd sat him down and tried to explain it to him. Besides, even sitting him down would have been a problem because, being pan dimensional, he didn't have physical form. Additionally, he certainly wouldn't have understood the concept of sitting. It would also have been difficult to talk to him about his views on the benefits and possible drawbacks of immortality because, like all his kind, having always been immortal, he knew nothing else. He had always 'been' and would have been totally unable to conceive otherwise.

Existing pan dimensionally was a tremendous advantage in his line of work, though he wasn't aware of the true scope this gave him. Unlike most of his kind he was an artist. He was rare in his choice of interest. Most of those he knew were philosophers and deep thinkers who conjugated for infinity on the true nature and meaning of existence. They metaphorically wrung their hands in frustration as they grandly genuflected on the limitless possibilities, which, as they had no frame of reference, was a pretty pointless endeavour. They ruminated fiercely amongst each other on the reasons that they were that which they were. Despite an eternity of debate they were bereft of answers. Evidently they *were* all that was, and no matter how potentially enlightened the exchanges between them became they were unable to see beyond this.

The artist preferred creativity. Though the concept of beauty was one that he could not have grasped, his creations gave him, and sometimes others, pleasure. Occasionally, when he'd allowed himself to go with his feelings, he'd create something that would give him pause for thought. He recognised this on the odd occasion when it happened. He recognized what he'd created made him feel 'different'. It was a hit or miss affair but when he struck gold it stood out. Thus his philosopher friends encouraged him. They all relished the altered state that one of his 'special works' could engender.

He unveiled his latest work with some trepidation. As far as he was concerned there was something special, something relevant about it; though relevant to what he couldn't even begin to conceive. His peer group studied his creation intently. It was interesting, it was complex and adventurous, yet there was balance. It had been thought through logically but it reached out in a way that gave them a frisson of excitement. They looked intently at the complex lattices weaving in and out of each other in a harmonious pattern, a pattern that incredibly embraced both logic and chaos simultaneously. The form of the highly organised possibilities and probabilities were based on random elements that gave it its uniqueness and yet it had a rigid structure that held together. It was as the work was studied more closely its impact and implications began to make themselves apparent. Whichever way they looked at it, it worked. It was dichotomy expressed as art. A unique achievement.

"You know, this is a breakthrough; there are possibilities here."

Gratified at the response to his endeavours the artist basked in their appreciation.

"Thank you," he said. "I'm going to call it 'time.'"

- The End -

MY SPECIAL GUEST TONIGHT

"Open that mother fucking safe or I'll blow your mother fucking brains all over this nice carpet!" shrieked the masked gunman as he pressed his gun into the temple of a portly middle-aged female bank clerk. Evidently he'd picked the wrong person to intimidate "Fuck you, asshole!" she screamed and brought her handbag up in a swift and surprisingly powerful arc, clipping the gunman smartly round the head. Falling back stunned, the man inadvertently fired his weapon. The bullet hit the ceiling and ricocheted though one of the bank's windows straight into the head of an elderly man driving cautiously down the small town's main street. His head exploded like an overripe tomato and he fell forward onto the steering wheel. The car careered out of control for a hundred metres then veered dramatically left into a graveyard, ploughed through a crowd of mourners and ended up, hood downward, in a newly dug grave, much to the astonishment of a priest who was about to conduct the burial.

The applause was rapturous. The lights went up in the studio and still the audience laughed and applauded. The chat show's suave and experienced presenter smiled a thin smile and addressed the camera. "And that, ladies and gentleman, was a sneak preview from *Killing Kids for Cash*, the latest work from that enfant terrible of new wave Hollywood, Tarquin Querrin. It's his follow up to the massively successful *Lets Torture the Bitch*, which the *New Yorker* memorably described as *'A triumph of nihilist deconstruction. Sexual politics with a switchblade, real blood and dark humour. Refreshingly brutal.'* I don't know what it means Ladies and Gentlemen, but here he is, the hero of the hour, to tell us all about it."

Tarquin grinned at his interviewer. Christian DeVille had the biggest chat show on the planet and was not to be underestimated. Christian's reputation as a keen intellect and a merciless interrogator did not faze him. He was basking in the glow of success. Four hit movies in a row. The studio would back him whatever he said as the big bucks he'd created rolled into their back accounts like a tidal wave. He was untouchable. His words and thoughts were valuable and meaningful. Had he not won two Oscars in row? Did not the biggest stars in the business fawn before him to read his profanity littered, pop culture dialogue? The word 'genius' had been used on a few occasions. He wouldn't dispute that. He knew what sold and relished his notoriety.

Christian started to move things along. "I must tell you, Ladies and Gentlemen, Tarquin nearly didn't make it here tonight. He had a car accident on the way to the studio but being the trooper he is he insisted on coming. Are you sure you're OK Tarquin?"

"Just fine Christian," he laughed back. "Just a slight ringing in my ears." Rapturous applause again exploded throughout the studio.

"Ask not for whom the bells toll Tarquin," observed Deville dryly, then he started. "Why do you like violence so much?" The question came out like a whiplash.

Surprised by the interviewer's tone but unfazed, Tarquin relaxed into his well-worn patter. "In a world numbed into boredom, violence is the new intellect; it cleanses and focuses the psyche. And, let's face it. It can be funny. For example, remember the scene in *Slaughter High* where the cheerleader stabs the principal in the crotch with his own letter opener? It's got everything. The realisation of teenage angst, a young girl emerges into true womanhood by a positive act of showing a mature man that she's not to be oppressed, and her comment 'That's for my grades,' is genuinely funny."

The audience clapped in unbridled enthusiasm as they recalled the now famous scene, a scene made even more memorable because the cheerleader was played by an actress previously famous for her 'good girl' roles. She'd done everything to get the part and the credibility that it would give her as a serious actress. Tarquin mentioned this fact to Christian who responded, "Why does that scene make her a serious actress?"

"It's about empowerment Christian, don't you see?" replied Tarquin cheerfully, warming to his subject. "In the movie she's empowered by what she does and, off screen, she's empowered by the success of what she achieved in the movie. This just shows, as I've always said, violence can be a positive force. It just depends on how you look at it."

"How about from the point of view of the victim?" the interviewer replied almost absent-mindedly. For the first time in many years Tarquin realised he was confronted by someone who was not following the adoration line. He was about to speak when his interrogator asked, "Have you ever experienced real violence Tarquin?" The audience quieted eager to hear the reply. The director was aware that the studio seemed to be getting uncomfortably warm.

"Christian, it's well documented that I never discuss my private life, my movies talk for me," he responded with a conviction he didn't feel. "Ah, I see," replied the interviewer, stroking his chin thoughtfully and continuing, "So you write about violence because you know it makes you money. And as you've never experienced it, you feel that it can be funny?"

Uncomfortable with the line in questioning but still relatively unruffled, Tarquin responded. "I didn't create violence. Violence is all around us. I merely reflect society and put a humorous twist on it. I'm a mirror if you like, and I give people what they want, that's why they go to see my movies."

"Ahh," murmured Christian. "You deny that your work influences people?"

"Absolutely," Tarquin responded.

Looking through his notes Christian continued. "It says here that you have said, on the record, that you were influenced by *A Clockwork Orange, The Wild Bunch, Dirty Harry, The Texas Chainsaw Massacre, Deliverance...* shall I go on?"

"Yes but that was creatively," Tarquin responded.

Christian pressed his point. "Your creativity is expressed through the scripts you write, but does it concern you that those who cannot write scripts may manifest these influences in other ways?" The audience was now totally silent.

Tarquin tried to marshal his thoughts. God, it was hot in this studio. "Look, if people get the message that violence is acceptable from these movies then that's not my fault." he blustered.

"So you accept the fact that your work can have an affect on others?" snapped Christian. "But you'll gladly take the money no matter how much damage you cause." The last comment was a statement.

The auteur made to reply but it was a difficult question to answer, difficult because Deville had got him cornered and he had started to feel decidedly unwell. His head started to pound. The accident must have affected him more than he imagined, "I...I...you know, it's awfully hot in this studio Christian."

Christian was solicitousness itself. "Oh Tarquin, I'm so sorry. There's you not feeling too good and I'm giving you a hard time."

His head banging, Tarquin fought to keep his eyes in focus as Deville's calm voice enveloped him. "I didn't know you didn't like my movies," the director mumbled.

Deville's eyes flashed with purpose. "Oh, but I do, Tarquin, oh but I do. In fact I love them...they're right up my alley. I select my show's guests very carefully. It's not easy to get in front of me but now I'm convinced you had what it took to get my attention...I had to be sure you see?"

Now, definitely feeling extremely sick, Tarquin was aware of dampness on his shirt. He looked down at it, trying to focus. His whole torso was soaked with blood. He made to cry out but no words would come. He tried to move, but his movements were sluggish as if his body was no longer his. In blind panic he looked up. The studio audience was nowhere to be seen. Only Deville remained, studying him from his chair.

"Goodness Tarquin, that accident must have been worse than you thought," he said, and got up from his chair. He pulled Tarquin up with a surprising strength and started helping him across the now empty studio. Holding onto him for dear life, the director mumbled, "I didn't think it was that bad at the time."

"Yes I know," replied DeVille. "It often happens that way. But don't you worry, I'm going to make sure you get extra special attention."

By now they'd reached a door at the far side of the studio. "Here we are," murmured the interviewer. He opened the door and Tarquin felt a rush of heat and saw flickering flames. DeVille roughly pushed the director through it. "See you shortly," he said, then gently closed the door and paused briefly to pull a bright silk handkerchief from his pocket.

He bent over and wiped the dust off an inscription in gothic script on the door: *Abandon Hope All Ye Who Enter Here.*

- The End -

DEITY

When he first found out it had been quite fun. He'd been too young to find it scary or even awesome, such is the capriciousness of youth. Though now elderly, he could still, understandably, recall the exact moment the differences between himself and everyone else manifest themselves. He'd been standing on a school rugby field on his thirteenth birthday.

As a gangly youth he had scowled into the wind, bemoaning the wretched weather, his maths teacher, his raging acne and pretty much everything a pubescent teenager has to contend with. The cold rain lashed down as he shivered and walked miserably over to take his place in the scrum. He growled under his breath, "Stop bloody raining," and it did…just like that. His mood prevented him from linking his comment to the change in the weather. From his place in the second row of the scrum he pushed and shoved, but the opposition was holding firm. Someone kicked his shin bringing a flash of anger to the surface. "Move!" he shouted, and immediately the opposition's front line started loosing ground dramatically.

When the ball came loose he broke from the scrum and hung back behind the line of play, willing it to be passed to him. It was. He ran with it for all he was worth. All he could think was, 'I'm going all the way.'

He knew it. As he ran he felt an empowerment that he'd not known before. Looking toward the rapidly approaching line he saw the imposing hulk of one of his particularly obnoxious classmates. A huge, squat and unattractive individual carrying significantly more weight and less brain cells than him. There was no way he could force himself past this guy. No, he decided in that instant…nobody was going to stop him. As his feeling of empowerment increased he thought, 'I'm going to hit this guy like an express train and he's going to go over like a bowling pin,' which is exactly how it happened. When he'd touched the ball down for the try he turned to see his enraged and bloodied classmate advancing toward him with fire in his eyes and bunched fists. 'I'm going to knock him out with one punch,' thought the victorious try scorer and, inevitably, that's exactly what happened.

In between the trials and tribulations of normal teenage existence he eventually joined the dots and considered the opportunities. All he had to do was to state what he wanted and it happened or he got it. When the inkling of what was going on began to occur to him he started with little things. A good exam result here and there, an instant respite to his acne and increased athletic prowess. By his fourteenth birthday his requests had matured a little, though only a little. Whilst he'd increased his intelligence level and therefore his exam results, he'd also taken delight during a routine physical in stunning the school doctor with the size of his penis. "Never seen anything like it," the old man had murmured unsteadily in the staff room over coffee.

As he sat in his rocking chair he smiled as he reminisced. The memory put him in a jovial frame of mind. It had taken him until he was eighteen to fully realise that he was a God. Not the God perhaps but certainly a God. "Let there be tea and current buns," he chuckled and, as he tucked in, he continued his reveries.

The eighteen-year-old God was certainly a very different individual from the pale thirteen year old who had stood on the rugby pitch five years previously. He was now tall, impossibly handsome and rich beyond the dreams of avarice. By the time he'd reached sixteen he was banned from every bookie in the country. Luckily the same constraints were not prevalent in the stock market. His fortune just grew and grew. Nor was he selfish with his requests. Much to his doctor's dismay his father went from a wheelchair bound asthmatic to a marathon runner almost overnight. To his father's amazement his mother regained the looks of someone thirty years younger while he'd been out for a game of golf.

Of course he tried to confide in his parents and indeed when he demonstrated a few tricks to prove his point they seemed impressed. Water into wine was always a good one, but bringing back the family cat that they'd all seen run over some years previously was a bad move. His mother became hysterical and his father bit off the end of his pipe. He did the only thing he could under the circumstances. He told them that they were to forget that he'd ever said anything and of course they did. He had the same reaction when he spoke to a priest. In retrospect he thought that the cleric's hysterical screech of "Get thee behind me Satan," had been a bit harsh.

So he kept his gifts a secret. His vast multinational holding company grew to the gross domestic product of a first world country. His power and wealth enabled him to bed the most attractive of women though his looks alone would have sufficed. The very few that weren't impressed were just told to find him irresistible, which they immediately did. He became bored, so he told himself he wasn't, then immediately he wasn't bored...until he was again. He'd considered issuing the instruction that he would never be bored again, but he realised that he'd be kidding himself and that his lack of boredom wouldn't be real. This was the first time that the young God had entertained an even vaguely philosophical thought.

By twenty-one he'd sold his huge empire. He ensconced himself in a sumptuous London apartment and read. He absorbed the great philosophers, the Bible, Buddhist teachings, the Koran...he sought the knowledge of the ages in order to understand what he was. A couple of weeks into his investigation he realised that the study was needless. He simply had to ask for ultimate knowledge and that's what he would get. So he requested it.

In that moment he was aware, with empirical experience, of the true nature of all things. When the revelation was complete he shakily muttered, "Let there be a bloody large gin and tonic," and took a big slug of it. Ultimate knowledge can be a heady brew for an immature twenty one year old.

In that nano second he understood that ultimate knowledge was limitless unless of course he chose that it was otherwise, which didn't really help him much. Nonetheless, what he had experienced of infinity was enough to make him realise it was a big place where anything was possible because that's what infinity was all about. Infinity, from what he'd found out, included just about everything. Opportunity, distance, time…the whole scheme.

His next request, born out of desperation more than anything, was the only command he'd ever uttered which he didn't believe would be answered. Respectfully clearing his throat, he demanded God's presence. A moment later, after an impressive light display, the smoke cleared and he found himself sitting opposite…himself. "No," he said, "I mean *the* God, not a God." "Same thing old chap," his alter ego replied. After a rather fractious discourse his doppelganger vanished, leaving him with the knowledge, in no uncertain terms, that he was God and that was the end of it.

As days go, it was a challenging one for the young man. Learning that he was the creator of all things brought with it a measure of responsibility which he decided to address assiduously. He waved his hand and, at a stroke, rid the world of all known disease and insisted that all guns on the planet would no longer function. Considering that he'd ended a day on a high note, he took to his bed.

Two weeks later most of the Middle East was running rivers of blood with hand-to-hand combat in the streets, as was most of Africa. Old scores were being settled with a vengeance. A month later there was rioting in most of the civilised world as the pharmaceutical companies, hospitals and arms companies laid off vast numbers of staff. Stock markets plummeted and prices skyrocketed. 'Opps,' he thought, and immediately changed everything back to the way it had been.

And so it went on. His overnight cure for Aids caused a population explosion and a resultant famine in Africa. His creative command that cars could run on tap water engendered traffic congestion that simply meant that societies ceased to function and whole economies collapsed. So he stopped interfering. He took himself off to a small cottage and lived a normal life and even allowed himself to grow old. Even if one had ultimate understanding, he reasoned, you could never predict the outcome. Naturally he could command an outcome but if he did where would free will and choice be? If he interfered that would make him a dictator and not God. People, he had learned, were not to be manipulated at his will even with the best of intentions, even if he was God. As he rocked on his chair he smiled to himself in the knowledge that he had at last learned wisdom.

- The End -

SCIENCE FICTION

He shivered at the chill and gazed out at the seemingly endless vista of rich pasture before him. The cattle moaned to each in early morning greetings. The twin sun's weak rays pierced the low clouds, creating a strange half-light in the clinging mist. It was hard to conceive of the unimaginable violence of a star ship arrival at times like these. Everything seemed so peaceful. Moving slowly towards the waterhole the animals regarded him through soft eyes. He inwardly sighed. This serene tableau was far removed from the gut wrenching reality of his existence; Politics, pressure and occasionally, treachery. He tried to hold on to the moment, only to realise that as he tried to grasp it, it danced playfully away from him like the end of a rainbow. He groaned as his communicator crackled into life.

"We have an inbound on the net. Please be advised that the err, Christ, I can't even pronounce its name, incept departure point Ursa Magellan, will acquire planet fall at 07.27 standard reference time. Access velocity is light speed times a sigma variable. Quantum flux indicates pre stage breaking procedure initiated. Expect maximum atmospheric disruption. Occupants, twelve crew and fifty passengers, all triple Y chromosome silicone based Argon breathers...not exactly a party crowd. We're gonna need rigorous immigration containment. We'll need the population in shelters by 07.00...this is going to be a rough one...it's a fast sucker and big...we'd better buckle up."

Managing this sector of the quadrant had been a huge promotion. God knows how many parsecs of celestial real estate came under his purview. That in itself was a big enough responsibility. His job was not made any easier by the fact that he was at the very edge of the Empire. They didn't call it an Empire of course. That was politically incorrect but, to all intents and purposes, it was an Empire and a prosperous one. Even more reason to police its outskirts with a robust and protectionist attitude. The Empire looked after its own. That was the reason for its existence.

His unfortunate geographic position meant that his sector was the first entry point for visitors from outside. This presented numerous headaches and challenges. Firstly, there were the inevitable customs and immigration formalities, which were a nightmare with some of the more exotic species that chose to visit. Protocol and courtesy were relative things. Trying to get across the nuances of bureaucracy and administration to visitors was a challenge. Visitors who were sometimes so different they were not recognisable as life forms at all. The last lot, as far as the sensors could ascertain, did not literally exist in real space-time and communicated via binary impulses only detectable in super heated plasma. Thank God he had a competent team of translators. He marvelled at the fact that their burn out rate wasn't higher. Talk about stress.

The second tiresome challenge was provided by the nature of space travel itself. Due to the unimaginable speeds ships had to travel to cover interstellar distances, slowing down was a problem. Good old-fashioned gravity offered a solution. Binary stars provided a gravity well that did the trick very well. These often exotic craft came shrieking in at huge multiples of light speed, aimed for the middle of the perfectly placed twin suns and let Isaac Newton do the rest. It worked very well, save for the shock waves it sent out over the surrounding few millions of miles causing huge disruption. The population needed to take to shelters to protect them from the shockwaves, as did the multiplicity of livestock that grazed the vast plains of his base of operations. Essentially the planet had to stop work for a few hours every time a ship arrived.

Inevitably of course, on occasion a colonist was caught outside. Normally some dim witted, idealistic frontier dweller who'd forgotten his communicator. And when it happened there was always hell to pay. Insurance companies asked questions and the paperwork backed things up for weeks. Still, the job paid well.

His sensitive location ensured that the operation never ran smoothly. 'Rumour Central' was its nickname. The shifting politics of the Empire and its repercussions were never far from his door. Though it purported to be a democracy, huge block votes from the wealthier systems ensured the continuity of power of those with vested interests. Inevitably those with less wanted more and those with more held on to what they had. Consequently uprisings occurred, civil violence occasionally flared up and the vast trading houses plotted each other's downfall with razor like precision.

His spaceport heaved with the flotsam and jetsam of society. Traders exported their wares, colonists eked out a meagre existence on the land, spies of the Empire plied their murky trade and exotic visitors from outside plotted sedition.

God, this was good stuff. Really original. He stopped typing for a moment and hit the spell-check. He particularly liked the section about how the Starships slowed down. It was clever; he could really make something of that. His science fiction was for the thinker. His intellectual affectations persuaded him that he had a duty to make his readers think. That was of course when he actually had some readers. As yet his writing prowess had yet to be fully appreciated. Actually, it hadn't yet been appreciated at all. It would be of course. The market was right for a more intelligent approach.

A 'ping' on one of the many screens surrounding the astronomer took his eye away from his recreation. He mentally jumped from the fantasies of the distant future to the mundane realities of radio astronomy in the twenty first century. He glanced at the readout: a gamma ray spike. Somewhere in deep space, a star had exploded with unimaginable violence. Since God knows when, the ripple in space had travelled from its distant origin to the warm sands of the New Mexico desert, a desert where he now sat surrounded by vast radio dishes listening to the sounds of infinity.

Gamma ray spikes were not unusual though they had been more frequent of late. If he'd have bothered to check he'd have noticed that their rate was accelerating but he was too immersed in his own fantasy world to bother. The powers that be, whilst recognising his technical competence, also recognised his lack of ambition and had assigned him the graveyard watch at the back end of astronomy.

His spotty assistant arrived in the room in a flustered manifestation of body odour, frizzy hair and unbearable enthusiasm. "We've got a new spike," he offered with tiresome energy. The astronomer stared bleakly at him with hooded eyes. "Log it in and file it," he murmured. Gamma ray spikes were hardly anything to get excited about. Radio astronomy was about a lot more than that. His superiors agreed. That was why they had him on the night shift. 'A lack of imagination' was the phrase that they'd used. It still grated with him. Imagination he had by the bucket load. When his flights of fancy were published, they'd show him to be the towering intellect he knew himself to be.

"You know we've been getting an awful lot of these spikes recently," gushed the assistant. "I ran an analysis earlier on. The sources seem to be getting closer. It's almost as if they are, well, coming our way. The algorithms hinted at what could be seen as a pattern."

The astronomer scoffed. "A pattern? Getting closer? Where did you go to school? The only thing that causes Gamma Ray spikes like this are exploding stars. Please feel free to commit career suicide by suggesting there is some cosmic phenomenon at work. Be my guest. Now, if you don't mind, I've got some real science fiction to write."

He was right of course. It was a ludicrous thought. To even suggest that the exploding stars were anything other than a natural occurrence was career suicide. It was unthinkable. Indeed, there were those who counted on such complacency.

The astronomer re read his most recent paragraph and basked at his own inventiveness. In that moment, every celestial monitoring device in the facility started urgently chattering out data.

The vast alien fleet appeared from nowhere just beyond the rings of Saturn. In a few short moments, in an explosion of stellar magnitude, their weapons blasted the Earth to oblivion. Pausing momentarily to confirm that no life forms existed elsewhere in the Solar System, they moved swiftly on to continue their conquest of the galaxy.

- The End -

CHANCE MEETING

It hadn't been the best of days. His boss had been a nightmare. He'd lost his cell phone yet again and now it was raining. As ever, the citizens of Manhattan showed their worst side as the deluge soaked him; the competition to find a cab only one step away from anarchy. He gave up the struggle and stepped into a Starbucks. The sudden change in temperature immediately fogged his glasses. He cursed himself for not picking up his new contact lens prescription. If that SOB of a boss of his hadn't buried him with work he'd have had time to do it. He cursed himself again that he didn't have the courage to stand up to him. Not that it would have made any difference. He'd probably get fired if he did and good jobs were a rare commodity in this town. Not that he had what he considered to be a good job but it paid well. A good job, as far as he was concerned, was one where you enjoyed what you were doing. Mick Jagger, now he had a good job. He was sure that George Clooney enjoyed getting out of bed most days, and he doubted that Tiger Woods ever had problems with the boss.

Not that he envied their lives, at least not too much. But he knew that they wouldn't have envied his. He wasn't actually poor and he was successful in his way but that was about the sum of it. Thirty beckoned in three weeks and this wasn't how he thought it would turn out. He reached for a tissue and wiped his glasses. As he replaced them he made for the counter and placed his order.

Nursing his tall latte, he walked to the last free table. As he sat down he looked at the other occupants of the establishment. He accidentally made eye contact with a woman at the table opposite. As he was about to smile she looked away, disinterested. Was it not ever thus in this city?

Frustration rose up in him. He had so much to offer. He was so much more than a number cruncher. He wrote poetry. Good poetry too. Not that his opinions were shared by New York literary agents. He was pretty proficient on the piano too. He wrote songs, ballads full of meaning and emotion. He spent hours refining his lyrical prose to reflect his thoughts. Not that anyone other than him had heard them of course. His offerings had been returned unopened by the music companies, with sharp notes informing him that they didn't listen to unsolicited material. He was kind, compassionate and sensitive but no one seemed to care. Oh, he'd had dates since he moved to the city but the rapaciousness of New York women just steamrollered his sensibilities. The ones he found interesting discarded him like used tissues, actually, most of them discarded him like used tissues, sometimes in mid date.

Not that he was unattractive. He modestly considered himself to be not less than average looking. He was in shape, still had his hair and was in possession of all his faculties. And, when given the opportunity, he was a good lay, but it rarely got to that stage. He was a considerate and imaginative lover. It wasn't ego. He knew this to be true of him. Why other people couldn't see his redeeming features was a mystery. Happiness appeared to be so easily achievable for others. It seemed that others had something that he did not but he was too intelligent to think this was really the case. He was a nice guy but he wasn't a wimp. Notwithstanding this it seemed his life was in the ultimate rut. Nothing he did or said seemed to make a difference to the way his life developed. As he considered these thoughts for the millionth time he was once again at a loss for answers. Could it be that none of his talents were enjoyable or worth anything unless he shared them with others? Did they actually mean anything if they were never expressed? It seemed he had all the gifts necessary for happiness. All the basics were there. It was as if he was poised on the launch pad, waiting for ignition.

The rocket's fuse was irrevocably lit by the woman who interrupted his thoughts. Asking him if he could share his table, she sat down before he could reply and launched into a tirade of abuse regarding the city he now called home. Her colourful language forced a smile to his lips as her invective brushed a number of his own touch points. She tore open her sugar sachets with venom and fixed him with a stare. "So what's your story?" She'd snapped, with a hint of a smile.

And that's when it happened, when his life changed.

She was a little older than him, probably the just the wrong side of thirty-five but very striking with it. Not traditionally beautiful, but blessed with such an excess of character he hardly noticed. On that first day she had interrogated him so rigorously he found himself laughing out loud at the onslaught. As he'd laughed, she'd laughed with him, seemingly realising the reaction her insensitivity had caused but enjoying it nevertheless. He had never known anyone like her.

As the afternoon passed to evening she sucked information out of him as if feeding on it. He was bewitched. Here at last was someone who seemed to be appreciating all that he had to offer. In apparent return for her enjoyment of him she offered scintillating humour, outrageous observations and an insightful intellect. She seemed very wise. Within two hours of meeting her he had looked inside himself and was embarrassed at the conclusion. He liked everything about her.

It was the little things: the way she reached out and touched his hand to make a point; the way she said 'Bullshit' when he got ahead of himself; her genuine consideration of his opinions, and her painstakingly honest assessment of his views. In return, he was no fawning recipient. He challenged her sweeping generalisations and probed her as deeply as she did him, luxuriating in her robust responses.

Later, at his apartment, (no one was more stunned than he) he winced as she pronounced his first stumbling song as 'sentimental horseshit.' It took a good deal of persuasion to get him to perform a second, which also didn't meet with much approval. The third hit the spot. Her mood softened. "Now that's what I was expecting," she said quietly. That they'd made love that night surprised him. That his ministrations were so obviously and so utterly appreciated delighted him. He'd never seen anyone so comprehensively satisfied. In turn she was urgent and creative, shocking and thrilling him with equal measure with her outrageous sensuality.

The next five days were a blur. In between falling totally and deeply in love he attended meetings with music and literary agents arranged through her connections. His poetry was received with embarrassing enthusiasm and music companies seemed to be queuing up for his songs. Every moment he spent with her was a revelation, every night a voyage of discovery. Life was suddenly good and he was pleased to see that she revelled in every moment with him.

The woman smiled at her counsellor. "Yes, it was everything you promised. It was well worth the money."

"You'll be doing it again?" enquired the counsellor.

"You betcha," confirmed the woman. "It's just wonderful to feel so needed."

The counsellor looked across the pristine uncluttered surface of her desk. She tapped rapidly on a touch sensitive screen in front of her and studied the data carefully then offered, "You put most of this together yourself didn't you? Well done. Most of our first timers take advantage of our consulting services to help construct a play scenario. Are you sure you want out now?"

The woman laughed. "I'm not made of cash you know."

Smiling, the counsellor fixed her with a steady gaze. "Are you going to tell him? We always recommend that you don't. Sometimes the guilt can have an adverse effect. It's best to let us handle matters."

The woman thought for a moment. "Yes, it's probably best that way," she murmured.

"Don't worry," said the counsellor, standing up and walking over to her. "It's company policy." She started to remove the electrodes from the woman's shaven head. "We always dispose of our client's sentient creations humanely."

- The End -

A WORK OF QUALITY

The editor looked at his watch with relish. Seven minutes to go. Seven minutes before he had to put up with that vile little man for the last time. That man whose very presence offended his sensibilities so deeply he felt the need to shower after their encounters.

He was going to cut him from the list and he was going to enjoy doing it. He'd not graduated a first in the classics at Oxford in order to read the wretched outpourings of a prurient scribbler. Writing was, after all, the great pursuit. It was an elegant and creative endeavour undertaken by conscientious and eclectic thinkers. People who wove their stories with skill and precision, artistes who played with language as a composer conducted an orchestra. Not that he wrote himself of course. He was an editor. His effete mind and intellectual snobbery persuaded him that he was able to critique that which he was unprepared to attempt himself. After all, he consoled himself, someone had to be the guardian at the gate. Someone had to ensure quality and high standards. And of course he did understood high standards. His lecturers had taught him well. He understood their exacting assessments and now their standards were his. He could accept no less.

Sadly, employment within the world of publishing was not the foregone conclusion he'd anticipated. After graduation he was astonished to have had to undergo the embarrassment of protracted interviews by individuals who were inferior to him in every way. And, they talked relentlessly about commercialism and profit which he felt was simply bad manners. Finally it took a quiet word from one of his former masters to a college old boy to ease his way into his chosen profession.

Four years in, he was relishing his environment. He savoured the ritual humiliation he was able to pour onto the new manuscripts that arrived on his desk. He took extreme pleasure in delivering his withering critiques to aspiring novelists and basked in the glow of his own importance as they thanked him for it. Yes, life was good. And now he was about to dispose of his most irritating author. He rubbed his hands in anticipation.

The man he was about to see wasn't exactly enamoured with the editor either. A seemingly modest and inoffensive character, he earned a living doing what he enjoyed most: writing horror novels. That alone was enough to pique the editor's ire. As far as the editor was concerned, it wasn't a genre, it was only a step away from children's comics and unworthy of his attention. When he'd ascended to his lofty position he was stunned to note that this author was still on their list. The reason he was became apparent from studying the records. The man's books sold just enough to turn a modest profit. Under the gentle tutelage and guidance of his predecessor the man had been just able to make the grade. Of course when he'd taken over his first task had been to undermine the writer relentlessly. He heaped scorn on his stories and attacked his grammar like a rapid dog. He studiously ignored phone calls and steadfastly subjugated the poor man to re write after re write. The resultant manuscripts were so poor they never had a chance. Even the man's most ardent fans drifted away.

His last book had bombed. The contract said that they had to at least consider one more. Certainly the editor mused, he'd consider it and then reject it out of hand. Problem solved. With the wretched man out of the way he could concentrate on more substantial works. He eagerly anticipated creating a withering torrent of invective when he gave his assessment of the soon to be delivered final manuscript.

The meeting was shorter than he'd expected. The man shuffled into his office reeking of cigarette smoke and slapped his new manuscript down on the table with a resounding thump. "You're not a very nice man," he said to the editor. "This is my last book for you. It's a work of quality; I wrote it especially with you in mind." Before the editor had time to laugh the man had gone, closing the door softly behind him.

Sitting down at home that evening in his favourite Chesterfield, he felt deep regret that he hadn't been able to execute the coup de grace himself. He felt somehow robbed. He vigorously stoked his fire and with a sniff of regret he lit a thin cheroot, took a sip from a large balloon of brandy and picked up the manuscript as if it were a used tissue.

Consoling himself this was the last time he'd have to endure the mans infantile and childish endeavours, he opened the manuscript with a heavy heart and started reading.

By the time he'd reached the end of page three, he felt his heart begin to race as his eyes scanned the horrific description being outlined in front of him. By the time he'd reached page ten his forehead was shiny with perspiration. He wasn't just shocked, he was revolted. The next two paragraphs were enough. He dropped the manuscript and ran to the bathroom, where he vomited. As he knelt before the toilet he felt rocked by the depravity he'd forced himself to read. When he eventually cleaned himself up he quickly poured himself another brandy. Christ, he had a legal obligation to read and critique this awful document. He steeled himself, sat down and again started reading. As he turned each page slowly wave upon wave of horrified fascination assailed his senses. He wanted to stop reading but he couldn't. There was something about the structure of the work that demanded he keep reading and yet the awfulness of the descriptions he was absorbing hit him like a sledgehammer. As his revulsion grew so did the dread, the dread of turning to the next page, the dread of reading yet another scenario laced with such primordial evil it made his flesh crawl.

By the time he'd read half of the book he'd also finished off the brandy. With a shaking hand he lit his last cigar. He had to see it through. He rubbed his eyes trying to focus on the words before him. As they cleared he felt panic rise up inside as he turned to a new page. Each paragraph tore at his veneer of civilisation and challenged his ability to endure the prose in front of him. His concentration was total. He'd long since stopped going to the bathroom to throw up, it took him away from the book. He retched where he sat, hardly noticing the smell. He already realised, in the small part of his mind that was trying to hold onto realty, that he would be changed forever as a result of this document. The dread grew within him as he continued to turn the pages. He now stopped reading frequently to look behind him in the now darkened room. His clothes were soaked with sweat. He made to retch again but he was empty. The awfulness of the next few paragraphs threatened to overcome him. He burst into floods of uncontrollable tears at the depths of this naked obscenity. He stood up, shouting in outrage and fear. He looked fretfully around the room again then, sobbing with terror, he returned to the manuscript.

The horror storywriter looked at the new editor and thanked him for his time. He was a kindly scholarly type who knew how to stimulate talent. He was delighted the man had bravely decided to keep him on after his last few failures. Such a refreshing change after the previous incumbent's unexpected suicide. The writer was almost disappointed that the remains of his last manuscript had been found in the burning embers of the man's fire. Such a waste…and the only copy.

- The End -

THE HOTEL AT THE
EDGE OF FOREVER

At the sound of high heels on marble the bored bellhop looked up quickly. The rapidity of his response rewarded him with an uninterrupted view of the new guest as she made her entrance. Twenty years spent assessing the nuances of those he unctuously served enabled him to judge that this woman was not a big tipper but definitely a class act. Normally such an assessment would have made him lose interest immediately but he kept on looking. He had to. Her deportment demanded it.

The woman strode confidently towards the check-in desk. The look she gave the receptionist was designed to establish superiority in terms of femininity, beauty, unavailability and wealth. The receptionist, a striking woman in her own right, was immediately intimidated. The new guest noted this with no satisfaction; it was simply the way things were. It was the way they had always been.

She snapped her black Amex card onto the counter, completed the signing in paperwork with deft brevity, turned heel and made her way to the elevator clasping a modestly sized Louis Vuitton overnight bag. The bellhop, who scurried over to her was halted in his tracks by her withering gaze and scuttled back to the concierge's desk like a nervous dog. 'Men,' she thought. 'Cowards or bullies'. She had no time for the former and she loathed the latter but was well able to use either if the need arose.

The suite was smaller than those in the cities she normally frequented. Nonetheless, she mused, it would do for the purpose at hand. She opened the door to the balcony and walked out into the blustery late evening. An uninterrupted view of the beach revealed an angry sea and an iron-grey sky. A few seagulls braved the elements and soared over the white tipped waves in search of food.

She surveyed the bleak scene without the slightest hint of emotion, then returned to the suite. As she entered she caught sight of herself in a full-length mirror and gazed approvingly at the refection. At thirty-six she had a figure that would have been the envy of women half her age…and normally was. Her clothes, studiously understated, reflected one of Giorgio Armani's more inspired days, and the application of her make up would have challenged the most professional of artists. She turned away bored, the brief uplift of seeing her reflection now lost.

She picked up a hotel brochure lying on a low table next to an extravagant bowl of fruit. She was briefly annoyed that she couldn't quite read the name of the town in which the hotel was located. That she couldn't identify the town was not the cause of her annoyance, it was the fact that she presumably needed an eye test and was perhaps less perfect than she desired. She picked up the phone.

The receptionist's bright tone answered. The woman enquired the name of the town. When the receptionist responded the woman couldn't quite make it out. Upon asking again she had the same difficulty. Not wishing to appear anything less than in control, the woman snapped a curt "Thank you," and replaced the receiver. She still found it strange that she didn't see the name of the town on her way in. She consoled herself it had been a long drive.

She picked up her overnight bag and made to put it on the bed, and froze. A sense of unusually strong déjà vu assailed her senses. So powerful was the experience she was rooted to the spot. The doorbell rang. She knew it would.

Feeling slightly apprehensive (a rare occurrence for her), she strode across the room towards the door. Still in the grips of déjà vu, she knew a tall man would be standing in the doorway. She hesitated for a second, then, gathering her confidence around her like a cloak, opened the door. Indeed, a tall man stood in the doorway. She had no idea who he was. The man, on the other hand, seemed to know exactly who she was. Without a word he threw her a quick nod then walked directly across the room and out onto the terrace. Like the woman, he showed not the slightest emotion as he surveyed the dismal scene.

She shut the door quietly, picked up an orange from the bowl and wandered out to join him. The man continued to scrutinise the horizon and seemed oblivious of her presence. Unused to this sort of treatment, she felt vaguely anxious, cross and unusually out of control. However, nothing on the surface gave even the slightest hint that anything was wrong. She leant nonchalantly against one of the posts supporting the balcony above, rubbing one of her arms with an immaculate hand in an effort to keep warm, whilst smelling the orange she held in the other. She affected a slight smile with a hint of a raised eyebrow in case he should decide to turn around. She desperately wanted to get the control back. A man walking into her room without speaking to her wasn't going to get the better of years of self-control. In fact just thinking about it in such simple terms enabled her to see the ludicrously theatrical side of what was happening. She felt the power surging back into her and was once again thankful for 'a good head on a good body'.

The man chose this moment to finally turn around but instead of speaking to her, he made a small gesture showing that he was beginning to get cold and re-entered the room. 'Alright,' she thought, beginning to enjoy the game, 'Let's see who's best at it'. She knew how to walk, she knew how to hold herself, she knew how to get attention and she put all of this knowledge into action during the short time it took her to re-enter the room, drop the orange on the bed and cross the room to the bathroom. The man, already sitting in the leather armchair in the corner with crossed legs and joined fingers, the tips of which just covered his mouth, took no notice of her. He didn't even follow her with his eyes. He appeared deep in thought.

She suddenly gave herself a mental slap round the face. Who was this man and why had she let him so calmly intrude on her space? Why was she even making an attempt to dally with him when she didn't even know him? There was a reason that she'd come to this place. It was remote enough for her to do what she had to do with no interference. Men didn't affect her this way. They were one thing in her life over which she had total mastery. She was giving this intruder her time and he wasn't even paying her for it. As if sensing her frustration, the man murmured, "Alors, comment c'était cette fois?"

"What?" she said. "Oh I'm sorry," he replied, "It's English this time, isn't it? What I asked was, 'How was it?'" "How was what?" she replied. "All of it, this time around," the stranger replied making an extravagant hand gesture indicating huge scope. As he gesticulated, she again had the powerful sense of déjà-vu. She knew this man...really knew him, but she couldn't place him. "I know you," she stated flatly. The stranger laughed. "I should hope so; still, you haven't answered my question."

She looked at him, really looked at him and he met her gaze full on. She saw a man in his late forties, very handsome in almost a Middle Eastern way but difficult to place. He wore a trench coat, an expensive one, which he had unusually buttoned up to the collar. His eyes bored into hers as she scrutinized his. She wasn't sure what she could see within them. Whatever it was it was calling to her in a way that she found most difficult to deal with. She knew men's eyes, but she didn't know his. The déjà vu persisted unabated and was reaching a stage where everything was beginning to feel unreal. She broke her stare and sat heavily on one of the chairs feeling dizzy. The stranger stood up with a smile, "It's never easy...I know...at least that's the way you always make it for yourself," he said.

Feeling too disoriented to talk, she gestured for him to continue. "Very well," he said quietly, "Do you really believe that a hot bath, a bottle of vodka and a razor blade are going to solve anything?" She looked up sharply. "How did you know?" she demanded. "It is my business to know," he continued. "It's what I do."

She took a deep breath and regained some of her composure. She stood up and smoothed down her skirt, then walked with some dignity to her overnight bag. "Whatever you think I'm going to do next, I need some of this," she snapped and pulled out a bottle of vodka. As she poured a shot into a glass, the stranger observed, "I'm not here to stop you doing anything; I'm just here to give you a little perspective."

Despite the bizarre situation the women still couldn't reconcile the fact that he appeared unmoved by her. This ability was the one constant in her life. Ever since she could remember men were the one thing over which she had total control. Certainly it had been a pleasant discovery when she edged into her teens, but it had soon become a burden. She eventually recognised the uses of her gift and the financial opportunity it afforded her to lead the life of luxury she thought she craved. As time moved on, her loathing of men increased as did the quality of her lifestyle. There had been one or two individuals along the way, men who had managed to keep up the pretence of not being intimidated by her femininity and beauty, but their facades had eventually crumbled into what she hated the most: adoration.

Not so with this strangely familiar man. Her experience told her that he most certainly wasn't gay, but the fact that he was uninterested was a jarring and unfamiliar sensation. She didn't like this feeling. Rejection or disinterest from a man was alien to her and deeply unnerving. It made her feel drawn to his dark beauty. She found herself wondering what he'd be like. Was this how men felt around her she wondered?

His voice pulled her out of her reveries. "So, to the matter at hand. If you want to kill yourself, please go ahead. I won't try to stop you. That's not how it works. It's just that it won't achieve anything, as you'll recall the minute you commit the act. As I asked you before, 'How was it this time?'"

"What do you mean 'this time'?" She asked, annoyed.

"Your life," he replied. "This is not the first time you've been here, and you've reached the same resolution every time. You must be getting a little bored of it by now."

She blinked at him in amazement. "I have no idea what you're talking about," she shot back.

"I'm familiar to you," he continued. "You feel it but you don't understand it. Indeed this whole situation is unnervingly familiar and yet you can't put your finger on it, can you? That's the way it's supposed to be. If you could remember everything you wouldn't get what you wanted from the experience. It's your gig, but you're alarmingly predictable. It's like you're stuck in a loop. I've tried to help. That's what I do but you're very difficult to reach once the game begins." He walked over to her. She found herself unaccountably trembling slightly at his closeness. 'Shit,' she thought. Up close he was seriously handsome.

"You're beautiful, rich and powerful," he continued. "That's exactly what you set out for yourself this time. It's what you set out for yourself every time but it always ends the same way. You cut your losses and break for the border. What you fail to realise…what you *always* fail to realise when you're here, is that what you seek is not dependant on these factors. You set these factors out for yourself for a reason. You gave yourself these gifts to provide a scenario, a scenario whereby you would have the opportunity to experience that which you desire to experience. I've tried to let you know in so many ways, but you're very focussed down here; you rarely hear."

She didn't fully understand his words but something within her told her that his bizarre monologue was in some way true. In that instant she made a brave decision. She dropped her guard a fraction around a man. For everything there is a first time she mused. "I don't know who you are," she confessed. "But I know I know you. I don't know how but I do. I'm tired. I'm bored. I'm disillusioned. I'm depressed. A quiet afternoon with a bottle of vodka in a hot bath with a razor seems a very appealing way to check out of this mess and stop the hurting."

The stranger smiled. "Progress, at last. In the past you've just ignored me and did what you felt you had to do. Somehow I've reached you this time. I know you don't fully understand what I'm saying, but believe me my only agenda here is you and that which you desire the most. If you do what you've done in the past and not listen then it starts all over again. Sure, the scenarios are slightly different every time, but the basic outline is the same. It's not till you start listening and noticing that you can make the changes necessary to get to where you want to be. *You* chose this scenario and *you* have to resolve it. Until you do you'll keep replaying it. That was *your* choice too."

She took a large slug of vodka and savoured the warmth rushing into her stomach. She was about to pour herself a second shot when the man, moving surprising swiftly, grabbed the bottle away from her. "I'd really rather you didn't. I need your total attention." She affected a mock pout, one of her best. The stranger didn't react at all. "You had my attention but you're talking in riddles," she said. "Just give me a straight answer. Who are you and why are you here?"

"I am here for you. That is sufficient. I cannot be more specific because that will ruin your careful plans. You were most definite about this. Look on me as a guide if you will, through a difficult maze of your own making. I'm always available if you let yourself look for me. Seek me out in the quiet places in your mind and you'll find me."

"More riddles," she retorted, but not quite so aggressively, "Look, you had what it took to get into my bedroom without reaching into your wallet. Believe me, you're experiencing very rare air. Yes, I do feel that I've done this before but we all get déjà vu."

"What do you think déjà vu is?" the man smiled." It's a crucial point in the game that has been important in previous playings."

"So," she said, "I've really done this before, but I don't remember it?"

"You don't remember it but you do feel it. Trust your gut. You know it to be the truth."

She'd given up trying to make an impression on him. Nonetheless, as she reached for a cigarette, she couldn't help but arch her back in manner designed to cause notice. The man smiled kindly. Not the reaction she'd ever engendered before with one of her moves. "What was the best moment of your life?" he asked.

Surprised by the question a moment popped into her head. As she was about to speak he cut her off. "No," he said. "Really think about it. A moment when you were truly happy, when everything was just right. A moment when you knew you were loved. A moment that you loved. A moment when time seemed to stand still and you wanted to hold onto that moment forever. Dig deep inside yourself and tell me about it."

His voice was so sincere she did as he asked. She closed her eyes and tracked back across the years, until she summoned up an event that she thought she'd long forgotten. The recollection of the long dormant memory stunned her with its power. She spoke, hesitatingly at first, then faster as she relived the experience.

"My tenth birthday. My parents surprised me by waking me up together. My mother kissed me. I can remember her perfume, she always wore Dior. I sat up in bed rubbing sleep from my eyes and then my dad hugged me. I remember his face was always shiny in the morning because he'd just shaved. I used to call it his smoothy face. When my dad pulled away my mom reached down by the side of the bed and picked up something. She told me to close my eyes and when I did she placed something on my lap. I opened my eyes and saw the most perfect kitten." She paused, the emotion welling up inside her. "I picked her up and held her to my face. As I buried my face in her, my mom and dad hugged me together. I could smell all of them. I loved them so much I could have burst and I knew that I was loved in the same way." She stopped, overcome. She felt the tears welling up inside her.

"I feel so silly," she choked, "but I wanted that moment to last forever." She tried to maintain control but the power of recollection threatened to overwhelm her. Embarrassed, she stood up to grab a tissue and in that moment the stranger held her. He embraced her as she allowed herself to let go. She cried for the loss of that long ago moment. She cried for her frustration. She cried in remembrances of a feeling that she hadn't even realised that she'd forgotten. As she sobbed she was shaken to realise that there was an ecstasy in this release. Her barriers were down. She was raw emotion. She recalled unconditional love and the nirvana of the timeless moment.

As the stranger held her, he gently smoothed her hair. "This is what this is all about," he murmured, "This is a hint of what you wanted to experience. The harder it is to get here makes the moment even more special. You gave yourself some tough barriers. You're very brave but you insisted on the full nine yards. The door has been opened slightly. You can build upon this. The emotions you feel right now are the only reality. You wanted to forget them so you could experience the bliss of re discovering them. It's the work of heros."

A cigarette later, the woman looked at her mascara-streaked face in the mirror. Normally she would have reacted in horror. Instead, she laughed, a deep, rich, vibrant laugh that had the stranger chuckling as well. "Impressed?" she said.

The man stood up and grinned. "I've told you all I can. I've helped you have a peek at what's going on. You've got to work the rest out for yourself. Your rules, remember? You know where to find me." He turned and made for the door.

She moved quickly, blocking his path. "Don't go," she said. "I want to talk to you forever." "You have been," he replied gently.

"You're here for me right?" she chuckled. He nodded. "If I need something you're there for me, yes?" she continued. "In a nutshell," he responded. She leaned forward and whispered into his ear.

As she lay on the bed in the half-light, she looked through the gloom as he entered the bedroom. He leant over her and gently ran his hands over her perfect shoulders and breathed in her powerful scent. She shivered in anticipation as she caressed the white downy feathers of his wings.

- The End -

TOP SECRET

For the umpteenth time Lieutenant Colonel Chester 'Ches' Washington, United States Air Force, call sign *Bullseye,* suppressed a smile as he drove past a ragged group of deluded no hopers on the desert road that led to his place of employment. Bearing their usual banners of *'Aliens are here now'* and *'Show us the captured UFO's',* their amiable and enthusiastic haranguing almost made him feel affectionate.

He hadn't always felt so sanguine about the interest his place of work engendered. Both the mad and stupid, and sometimes, to his abject dismay, the very intelligent, often posed of him the sort of questions which made him want to hold his head in his hands and sob with frustration at their gullibility. Two years previously, when he'd been selected to continue his cutting edge flight testing at the very outer limits of flight technology, his posting to Groom Lake Air Force facility had been a dream come true.

He'd graduated in engineering from a respectable college and joined the Air Force. There he discovered the unique skills needed in handling the awesome challenges of flying a fast jet were something he possessed in almost embarrassingly large quantities. This, combined with his keen engineer' mind, came to the notice of the powers that be. After tours in Bosnia and the Gulf, the brass had encouraged him to take an Air Force scholarship to complete a PhD. Graduating top of his class, he was assigned to Edwards Air force base, the spiritual home of all test pilot elite. Like Yeager, Crossfield and Armstrong before him, for three years in the high desert he flew everything that was thrown his way. He tangled with the high concept experimental machines that were delivered from the legendary Skunk Works at Lockheed Martin and drawings boards at Northrop Grumman and others.

Noting with interest his flawless record of intelligent flight assessment and a flying logbook full of an astonishing array of aircraft types, the same generals who had encouraged him to take his doctorate conferred with shadowy colleagues in various government agencies, and a decision was made. Shortly afterwards, Chester Washington was invited to attend a meeting in the nation's capital.

There he faced various bemedalled and very senior military types, together with a number of unnamed civilians whose function seemed a little unclear. Nonetheless, they seemed enthusiastic about him and his career to date. Evidently a full and thorough investigation had been carried out on his background, above and beyond what was normal for his position, and he'd not been found wanting. Upon hearing this he immediately assumed that he'd been selected for some clandestine CIA sponsored activity. About to protest, one of the civilians held up his hand before he could utter a word. "Colonel, before you say anything, we'd like you to sign this," he offered and pushed a sheet of paper in front of him. It bore the legend '*Top Secret*' *Level C1/Majestic12/a51.*

Unfamiliar with the clearance level, he raised his eyebrows and again, just before he was about to speak, the same civilian spoke. "No, you won't be familiar with the clearance level, but suffice to say it'll put you in the top point one percentile of all cleared personnel in the US. That's a very small and select group Colonel. Only sign if you're prepared to be bound by it. Clearances don't really get much higher than this." Naturally intrigued, Chester signed it with a flourish and sat back awaiting God knew what.

A naval admiral leaned forward, cleared his throat and addressed the Colonel. "Now you've signed the document you can only ever discuss what we are about to tell you with the people in this room or with someone whom one of the people in this room has given you written authority to speak with. Is that absolutely clear?"

Somewhat taken back by the admiral's brusque manner, the pilot snapped back. "How am I supposed to get written permission when I don't know any of the names of the civilians here or what they even do?" An Air Force general smiled. "And it's highly unlikely that you ever will, Colonel. Let's just say, 'Don't talk about this briefing ever, unless it's to your next commanding officer who is similarly cleared...and yes, you can have that in writing...from me."

The admiral took over again. "Put simply Colonel, let me remind you of an old-but-true adage: 'Government is too important to be left to politicians'. No, it's not treason, it's a fact. Please, may I ask you not to interrupt me until I have completed my little speech? We're not here to debate this issue today, but to simply get you up to speed. For many years, very senior people in various arms of the military and various government agencies have ensured this country's and the free world's preparedness and superiority against all its existing and potential threats. Government, presidential or otherwise, is simply an administrative device for effective management. Democracy unfortunately makes this less efficient than it might be but we have to at least give an appearance of a free society. The people that really run this country, and indeed a great many others, respect and support freedom but we recognise that run rampant it would totally destroy itself and probably the planet as well. The great initiatives that have kept the population secure and safe have never been hatched by Congress. Indeed the really key decisions cannot be left to a bunch of squabbling, self-serving politicians. So we let them do what they do whilst wiser heads get on with it making sure things happen and work or sometimes vice versa."

Chester's face obviously betrayed his emotions. The admiral once again cut him short. "As I said Colonel, this is not a debate. For example, the B2 Stealth Bomber and the F-17 Stealth Fighter give us unrivalled air superiority. They enabled our Gulf War causalities to be held at a level unimaginable even a decade earlier. Our nuclear submarines are undetectable. The alloys used on our unstoppable smart missiles enable us to make them lighter and fit the targeting technology that makes collateral civilian casualties almost negligible. Look at economics. Western financial dominance is not as a result of corrupt CEOs managing their fiefdoms like personal bank accounts, but it's due to the vast and intricate computer programs developed by various covert agencies to manipulate world markets. All these developments, and believe me, many many more, were conceived, protected and managed by people like us and colleagues throughout the civilised world. This is how things really work Colonel. The people have their security under the umbrella of what they perceive to be a democracy, while we try to keep them safe, with no interference from lesser intellects. Oh, certainly congress may have approved the budget for, say, the Stealth Bomber, but do you really believe that the costs they rubber-stamped was what it really cost? You're way too intelligent to believe that. The real development and management cost of projects of this magnitude are in black budgets hidden well away from the eyes of civil servants. If they were published, they'd never be approved, and we'd end up a second-rate power and vulnerable from all sides with the consequent knock on effect to our economy."

The admiral stopped to light a cigarette. Chester noticed, most unusually, that no one objected. "Of course," the admiral continued as he took a long drag, "we're also putting vast resources into a cure for cancer." There were a few discrete chuckles from around the table.

The Air Force general took up the reins. "It's the same with threats. You probably think it's mainly militant Muslims, Columbian drug cartels, Iran, North Korea or the Russian Mafia that pose us the biggest danger. Believe me, there are far greater threats to our security that we have to manage and cope with on an ongoing basis. We have to do this in secrecy so as not to cause alarm, and give the illusion of safety so that people can go about their business in blissful ignorance."

Unable to keep silent any longer the Colonel spoke. "If I accept, for the sake of argument, and I mean for the sake of argument, you're not a bunch of intellectual power-crazed egotists, why are you telling me all this? I'm a test pilot, not a politician."

"Indeed you are Colonel, and you're a professional," interjected one of the civilians, "as are we, and we'd like your help. What do you know about *Project Aurora?*"

Taken aback yet again, Chester thought for a moment, then replied carefully, "rumours mainly. I've heard that it doesn't exist."

"You are correct," agreed the suit. "It doesn't exist officially. Unofficially it very much exists, and to date twenty-five plus billion dollars has been quietly invested in it and many billions will follow. This vehicle can fly higher and faster than anything even in the imaginations of design engineers in the aviation industry. When the programme is complete the machine will be capable of a performance envelope that edges into science fiction. It will be the ultimate reconnaissance vehicle. We'd like you to work on it. You'd be based at Groom Lake Air Force Base."

He let the comment hang in the air. He had the Colonel hooked, and everyone in the room knew it. They didn't make mistakes. Groom Lake was regarded in almost mystical reverence in the flying community. Shrouded in mystery and the source of the most outlandish rumours, Chester would have given almost anything just to have a peek over the fence. Even its official call sign was intriguing: *Dreamland.*

The admiral stubbed out his cigarette. "Yes, Groom Lake, or as our little fraternity refer to it, *Area 51.* Sadly, due to the goddamn internet and the fucking *X-files* so does just about every member of the public." Once again a low chuckle reverberated around the room. "And no, despite the supermarkets tabloid's hysterical assertions," he continued, "it's not a facility for retro engineering downed UFO technology, nor are there alien corpses there, and we most certainly aren't in league with extra terrestrials to abduct human specimens so that they can have probes stuffed up their asses. Though if I were able to arrange it I can think of a certain senator that I'd like to put on the list."

Three days later, after a particularly unpleasantly rigorous medical, Chester found himself in front of his new commanding officer. The CO, a hoary old veteran with hawk's blood in his veins, bade him welcome. A plaque on his desk displayed a cartoon picture of a round eyed alien with a red cross through it. Underneath the illustration were the words '*If you think you've seen an extra terrestrial.... YOU AINT! And that's an order'*.

Chester retuned the Co's handshake and picked up the plaque with a smirk. "My wife's idea of a joke," smiled the CO. "It's the burden we shoulder for working here. Even my teenage son doesn't believe we're just a flight test facility. He asked me the other day if it was true the Air Force had a Blue Beret downed UFO rapid recovery team."

"I saw that episode," grinned the Colonel, "I thought it was rather good."

"You'll have to cope with a lot of crap outside," confessed the CO. "I'm sure you'll manage. Truth is, we'll be keeping you so busy you'll be spending most of your time on the base. What did you make of the *Illuminate?*" Chester gave him a blank look.

"The board in Washington," he continued. "A spooky bunch but very, very powerful...and they pay well...we see them quite a lot here. Still, they never cause any problems and they ask very intelligent questions and our budgets are passed without a murmur. God knows how they do the accounting but it gives us unrestricted opportunity to play with some pretty exotic stuff."

Within a few weeks Chester had found out that the CO's take on the word exotic took on a whole new definition of the word. Strapped into the cockpit of the sleek and massive beast that was project *Aurora* he'd initially gazed warily at the multiplicity of sensors and probes that ran from the high-tech cockpit to various parts of his body. The flight operating manual was a document the like of which he had never seen. Numerous references were made to systems and avionics that were as yet still totally foreign to him. He'd never heard of a *bio sat interface* or indeed a *cranial transponder* and the section on the pulse wave detonation engine had made his head hurt. Nonetheless, as time went by, his intelligence and engineering background ensured that he began to form an operating picture of the mind-blowingly advanced machine that surrounded him. Two years later he knew the needle nosed monster better than he knew his own body.

He gazed lazily out of the cockpit canopy at the clouds many miles beneath him as he chased the sun across the roof of the world. Here at the very edge of space, the lack of air made for an almost totally silent ride. His bio implants tingled, gently letting him know that he'd just entered the next satellite footprint and that his telemetry was being received on the uplink. He mentally recognised this fact and the onboard systems, acknowledging this thought, cut the physical stimulus. A soft chime sounded inside his helmet indicating a non-scheduled radar contact many miles below. He glanced at the radar screen and the intelligent glass on his visor interpreted his two-blink instruction and prompted the computer. Three seconds later an automated voice resonated inside his helmet.

"Target is an F22 out of Edwards Air Force Base, seconded to NASA, undergoing high altitude trials. Threat level zero."

Chester grinned. The engineers had given the system a woman's voice. She always sounded, well, so unflappable. This was just as well as he'd not always felt that way himself as he'd come to grips with the highly-strung aircraft. Project Aurora was the first and only trans-atmospheric aircraft in existence. Constructed of composites of a complexity that were way beyond his understanding, the craft could withstand the brutal physics that accompanied mach ten speeds and the mind-bending temperature variances that resulted. With its revolutionary propulsion system, the machine could achieve sub-orbital altitudes for a short while and a normal cruising altitude that made him undetectable from the ground. Not that that made a difference to any potential threat. His speed alone rendered him uncatchable.

It was a perfect reconnaissance platform, except for the fact that the powers that be had also fitted a weapons system. The logic being, he had been told by the suited faceless civilians, that should the enemy ever develop a similar aircraft then it was vital to have offensive capability.

The chime sounded again in his earpiece, followed by a second more urgent note. Before he'd had a chance to even look at the radar screen the glass of his visor lit up with telemetry. It took him a full three seconds to accommodate the information imparted and he knew it must be incorrect.

"Computer, re-verify data and cross check." He mentally visualised the satellite currently tracking him and immediately the computer relayed the information he'd received to the orbiting vehicle to confirm the telemetry.

"Onboard systems confirm data, satellite tracking verifies," said the unflappable woman.

Chester barked into his microphone.

"Dreamland, this is Bullseye, we have an indicated bogie, inbound at... inbound at...it's an error...inbound bogie at 450,000 feet at mach 4, decelerating. Definitely an error. It's higher than me and slowing down.

His earpiece crackled into life.

"Bullseye, Dreamland, your contact confirmed. Move to intercept. Treat with extreme prejudice."

Stunned, Chester replied. "What? Say Again?"

There was a short silence. This time the CO's voice came on the line, urgent and insistent.

"Chester, no debate, this is a confirmed threat, bring that sucker down."

The Colonel's training took over. He hit the scramjets and felt himself pushed back in his seat as the aircraft leapt forwards. Keeping his left eye on the radar contact and his right eye on the aircraft status he thought, 'Jesus, it's still slowing down.' Anticipating his thoughts the aircraft spoke to him. "Weapons systems online, target range 38 miles, closing velocity mach twelve." Doing the mental maths he realised he had seconds to make a decision. "Acquire target and snapshot one through four," he said softly.

One point three seconds later the aircraft shuddered as four missiles streaked from their rails. The moment their tailpipes ignited the target stopped abruptly. Chester blinked. The intruder had gone from mach four to a total standstill, a physical impossibility. Two seconds later it started to accelerate upwards at an unbelievable rate. Not quickly enough however. A moment later the sky lit up as the sleek metallic predators found their target.

It was a de-briefing to remember.

The moment his aircraft gently edged to a halt, it was surrounded by armed personal wearing an insignia he'd never seen before. With some alarm, he climbed down from the cockpit to face his CO who was looking faintly embarrassed.

Some six hours later a livid Colonel sat in front of the men from Washington. The Naval admiral again lit a cigarette and leaned forward, preparing to speak. Chester cut him off. "You can put that fucking thing out for a start," he shouted. "I don't care who the flying fuck you are. You've kept me prisoner here for hours, no ones told me anything and I've just had to shoot something down and presumably killed everyone on board on the say so of my CO with about four seconds warning. What the hell was it anyway? Jesus, the thing was above me and slowing down for Christ's sakes! It stopped completely before I hit it. That's just not possible."

"Be quiet Colonel," snapped the Admiral, "Or I'll have you locked down for twenty four hours until you get a civil lip." Shocked at his tone, Chester took a deep breath. The admiral sucked on his cigarette and continued, "I'm genuinely sorry you've been kept incommunicado. It's taken a while to get us all here. I'm also sorry for the experience that you had today. You weren't ready. Our intelligence was faulty. No incursions were expected in this area for a while. Your training wasn't complete. Now tell us exactly what happened. Leave out no detail. Once that's done we'll give you the answers you want."

Three gruelling hours later, the pilot sat back exhausted from the barrage of questions that he'd fielded. "That's it," he snapped. "I want chapter and verse."

"We're at war," the admiral said quietly. "We have been for almost sixty years. When we last met we told you how things worked, why they work, why we and many others manage what's going on. We explained the reasons: to try and keep this fragile planet peaceful and safe for its inhabitants. I explained that we control the flow of information, fund what needs to be funded, manage the world's economies from afar and do what we can to maintain the ecosystem. There are those who seek to take this away from us."

A civilian took up the narrative. "As I'm sure you're aware, in 1947 there were stories of a crashed UFO in Roswell, New Mexico. The legend developed that alien bodies were recovered. It was naturally dismissed by the military as a weather balloon. Working where you do I'm sure you're no doubt aware that there are incredible myths about the government working on projects based on technology from crashed UFOs. There are a plethora of books in the media about people who believe that they have been abducted by aliens and been experimented on. At Rendlesham Forest in England there were highly detailed reports of a UFO landing near a top security RAF base. The stories go on and on. What I have to tell you now is…they're all true."

He let the statement hang in the air.

Clearing his throat rather obviously, the Colonel spoke. "You'll understand that I'm a mite sceptical."

"You shouldn't be now," said the civilian. "You've just shot down a UFO. That's what Project Aurora really is. An interceptor designed specifically for that purpose. They're vulnerable when entering the atmosphere as you've just found out. You were due to be fully briefed on this in the next few weeks before the next incursion was predicted."

"You mean all this alien stuff is real?" Chester's head was spinning. "We really are retro-engineering downed UFO technology? There really are people being abducted and having experiments carried out on them? What the hell for? Have we really conducted autopsies on aliens? I mean… what's real and what isn't? Why are we at war? Christ guys, I need a briefing."

The Air Force general interrupted him. "I'm sorry Chester, you got thrown in at the deep end unprepared. What's actually happening is a little more complex than is imagined, even by the rumour specialists on the net. What we know is that these incursions have been occurring for the last sixty years. The purpose of these incursions is intelligence gathering. A prelude to invasion." He leaned forwards to emphasise his point. "They're very careful," he continued, "and we rarely catch them, but we've had our fair share of successes."

Chester tried to clear his head, "What's all this abduction crap and medical experiments about then? Is that part of the intelligence gathering?"

The admiral drew heavily on his cigarette. "Not exactly Colonel. As my colleague indicated, it's a slightly more complex situation. You see, the technology we need to defend ourselves isn't exactly easy to come by, even by studying downed flying saucers."

Now totally fazed, Chester ran his fingers through his hair in frustration. "Then where did we get it from?"

"We have a pact," the civilian offered, "with the Greys."

"Who the flying fuck are the Greys?"

The door to the briefing room opened suddenly. Chester spun around and what he saw rooted him to the spot. The pictures he'd seen on the internet were remarkably accurate, though the alien was taller than he'd imagined. Other than that, the black teardrop eyes and the large bald cranium were as predicted. Totally naked, the being's skin glistened in the room's harsh lighting. "We are Colonel," the creature said. "Both of our races have a shared interest in this vibrant little planet of yours."

Chester watched transfixed as it made its way around the room to an empty seat. Nobody else in the room even blinked so much as an eyelid.

The alien clasped his hands together in front of him as a human would. "You see Chester, we're in league. Actually our races relationship is developing into…what's the word? Oh yes…a symbiotic one. Through necessity. Both races have something that they need from each other. We've reached an accommodation."

Chester finally found his tongue again. "So I haven't just killed a bunch of your buddies?"

The alien made a noise which Chester surmised was an approximation of a laugh. "No no," it said. "They were the bad guys. We call them the Blacks.

Their agenda is simply invasion, conquest and colonisation. When they first arrived you were helpless. We've helped you fight back, given you technology, intelligence on incursions, that sort of thing."

"That's very benevolent of you," the Colonel murmured, "Are you sending a bill?"

"You're already paying and have been for some time," came the reply. "The Blacks are barbarians but we're not. We're enlightened compared to your race and compassionate in our way. Unlike the Blacks we're not expansionists by nature but our home planet is coming to the end of its life. We've been seeking a new home for a very long time and, well, yours is a pretty unique little globe, though for some reason you seem to have been hell bent on destroying it."

The alien waved some of the admiral's cigarette smoke away from his face. "And you seem to be intent on destroying yourselves as well," he continued. "Your race is one of such opposites. You are capable of the most unbelievably creative thinking and yet you are individually dominated by fear and the pursuit of happiness through acquisition of material possessions. You represent such a dichotomy. This why we need to study you, you see. To enable us achieve a true compliance between our races."

"What do you mean…compliance?"

"To enable us to…migrate here…we cannot do it with our current physicality. We are too alien to survive here for very long. The only way that we can achieve our exodus is by taking the best of us and the best of you and essentially achieving a merging of our races. A hybrid race if you like. Your *Illuminate* here faced a difficult choice sixty years ago. Conquest and extermination by the Blacks, or a pact with us to achieve a merger between our two races for mutual survival. Of course it's a very difficult task requiring huge research. I'm afraid all those abductions and experiments are us. Casualties of war if you like. A small price to pay for survival."

"Casualties of war?" shouted the Colonel. He felt physically sick. "And you bastards gave them a free hand? To experiment on our own people?"

"Really Colonel," murmured the alien. "Please put this into perspective. Less than point one percent of your population has been affected in the last sixty years. There's been remarkably few fatalities, and we do our best to keep the suffering to a minimum."

"You've abducted over three million people to experiment on them? My God in heaven. What have you been doing to them?" The Colonel maintained control only with the greatest of difficulty.

The unblinking eyes bore down on him. "Unlike your race we haven't been torturing laboratory rats so that women can paint their faces in safety Colonel. We haven't even incarcerated anyone except for a few hours now and again. Abduction is generally a gentle process, whereby the subject is only vaguely aware of their surroundings and wakes in the morning for the most part putting the experience down to a dream. The experiments are far too complex to explain here, but essentially the main thrust of our work is genetics. We've spent a great deal of time studying your physiology in order to engineer human-grey hybrids. That was stage one. Stage two was introducing our own genetic material into unborn foetuses of pregnant women and studying the outcome. The few infants that survived show great promise that our objectives can eventually be achieved."

"Dear God," the pilot mumbled, "You've actually created hybrids? Don't you realise that once these...creations...make their appearance, your little games will be over anyway. People will never understand. There will be mass panic. Whatever the threat from these so-called Blacks you'll be seen as the invaders you are. There's no difference between you and them except for the fact that you're sneaking in through the back door."

A civilian cleared his throat. "Actually Colonel, it won't be like that at all. This has been thought through you know. As our guest here indicated, the Greys cannot live here with their current physiology. As a result the early hybrids don't look any different from us. Mentally though they are generally superior in many ways. Increased intelligence, more developed brain functions, faster reaction times, etc, etc. By the time the final version of the hybrids is developed, the majority of the human race will already be dominated by the Grey gene and far better prepared to accept the truth once it's revealed."

The admiral appeared slightly embarrassed. "We're grateful for your time Colonel," he said, "and for your contribution to this program."

The pilot stood up and leant over the table, "My contribution to the so called 'program' ends right now gentlemen. I resign."

The Grey met his stare. "I'm afraid your contribution is inextricably linked to the program. You see, you're one of our greatest successes. As an educated man you'll understand our need to fully evaluate our experiment. It's vital for us to know what has made you survive and flourish while others did not. The contribution you've made to the survival of our races is invaluable and will never be forgotten. A fitting epitaph surely?"

With that, a civilian opened the door to the briefing room. Moving fast, four armed soldiers entered followed by a man in a white coat nursing a syringe.

- The End -

THE MAN WHO THOUGHT HELL WAS A BREEZE

The Prince of Darkness stoked his beard thoughtfully. His subjects rarely ever had his personal attention after admission. Few merited that honour. Normally, after his well-worn greeting, new arrivals were dispatched to his team of trusted lieutenants for them to do what they did best. The new souls were almost like his children though he would have never allowed himself that almost romantic notion. He'd sowed the seeds in their life and they'd picked up the baton and run with it. He preferred to think of it as creating his own supply.

The majority of these arrivals ran through the normal tiresome gamut of pleading and sobbing before they were taken away. The very few that showed a bit of grit just lacked imagination. Their sobbing and pleading simply started a little later. Laughably, some even insisted they were there by error. He particularly enjoyed welcoming those. After an eternity though, they all seemed to merge in together. He rarely heard anything new. Until now.

What his most senior lieutenant was telling him now was indeed new and it had piqued his interest. He observed the ministrations of one of his numerous teams putting a recent arrival through an unspeakably brutal ordeal. The subject was laughing. "You know," muttered his lieutenant darkly, "We're just not reaching this guy." The Devil raised an eyebrow. "It's been a long time since I had a challenge. I may have to take a personal interest." He recalled this soul's arrival. It was unusual as he'd exhibited a total lack of concern. He knew it wasn't down to mental illness as they were spared his domain. He just assumed, like others, he'd be reduced to naked traumatised fear once he'd been introduced to what this place was really all about. Evidently, despite protracted and sincerely creative efforts from his best people, this hadn't happened. It was most odd. Curious even. Still, he mused, 'It's been a long time since I've had to dig deep.' "I'm sure I can think of something," he said to his lieutenant.

With a wave of his leathery hand he altered the torment and subjected the man to a barrage of agony and abuse that had his trusted aide blinking with admiration. "My Lord," he offered gratefully, "You are truly are the Master." His revered ruler allowed himself a smile. Admiration always went down well. It was a weakness that he allowed himself. He couldn't allow himself many; after all it was only his will that held the place together. He stopped the scenario, eager to hear the supplication and entreaties for mercy. A hollow laugh was what he received. His lieutenant looked at his Lord with dismay. The Devil felt a prick of…what was it? Embarrassment? Newly motivated, he brought down on the man a mind-bending assault of such exorable depravity and pain even his lieutenant had to briefly look away.

The man chuckled uncontrollably. "Bring it on man, I'm lapping it up. Is that the best you can do?"

Some time later Satan flopped into his favourite chair and mopped the sweat from his brow. It wasn't the heat causing his perspiration; it was the sheer effort that he'd put in. Unbelievably, the man actually seemed to enjoy the nameless degradations and misery he was being forced to experience.

Not one to admit defeat easily he plumbed his creativity in his search to inflect horrors beyond imagination and get the man with the program. He met with no success. He revisited the man's time from whence he had come and studied it carefully. The man had been hell bound almost since he was born. A genuinely revolting individual. Of course the Devil wasn't shocked, but was certainly surprised it had taken the man so long to get here. His subject had lived long enough to not only comprehensively break all of the Ten Commandments, but he'd also a good many others that the Good Lord hadn't thought it would be necessary to remind mankind of. The Almighty always did tend to underestimate how bad his creations could actually be.

A short while later his most senior people arrived with the subject who, most infuriatingly, was sporting a broad grin. "You took your eye off the ball man," he said, "You got old and careless. You think you're bad? Yeah, sure you were, back then. It's a whole new ball game now." His lieutenants looked aghast. To their dismay the man continued. "You've been down here too long. You think this is bad? Have you actually been up there recently? Pain? Bring it on. I lived it all my life. I was beaten black and blue from the day I was born. A good day for me was one where I was only kicked senseless. Hell, it was the only attention I got so I started enjoying it. Gotta say, it toughened me up. Guess I've got you to thank for that. Isn't all that your influence?" The Devil nodded quietly. "Well pal, you did a good job. Didn't have nothing so I took what I wanted and didn't let nobody stop me. In fact I liked it when they tried. Gave me the excuse to mess them up. After a while I didn't need an excuse. Hell, I was messed up so I figured why shouldn't they be? Got to enjoy it too. Really enjoy it. You know, the rush. Always knew I'd make it down here. I was looking forward to it. Did everything I could to make sure I made it. You did a damn fine job of screwing me up. Good work. The best. Trouble is you and this place. Big disappointment. This is a breeze. You're not past first base after where I grew up."

He'd heard enough. The Devil motioned his charges to take the man away. He was tired and, after all, he had eternity to break him. His lieutenants remained rooted to the spot. He looked up sharply.

The man who thought Hell was a breeze laughed. He addressed the lieutenants, "Get this sorry sucker out of my sight. I'll sort him out later. Right now I got some changes to make."

- The End -

THE HITCHER

As a teenager she'd called it 'Hitching'. To herself of course. She'd never told anyone about it. It was her secret and one that she guarded jealously. She feared losing it. That must never happen. She couldn't live without it. She wouldn't live without it. Now, in her mid twenties, she continued to enjoy her gift, too caught up in its magic to recognise the signs of her total and utter addiction. And like all addicts, enough was never enough.

When she'd nudged into her early teens, metamorphosing from a boyish rake of a girl into a body that was full of promise of what full maturity would bring, life had been the uncertain and cruel affair that comes with puberty. A body and a range of new emotions and experiences changing her almost by the day. Tooth braces and the unwelcome discovery of period pains hadn't helped her introduction to the onset of eventual womanhood. She had been miserable and depressed. And then of course there had been boys. Insensitive, unsophisticated, single minded in the pursuit of their own burgeoning needs, there couldn't be a less endearing creation than the male in his early to mid teens. At least that's what she thought then. Now, more experienced, she realised that they did have their uses. An unbridled enthusiasm and a much-appreciated stamina were benefits that sometimes made up for their painful emotional immaturity and lack of experience. Not that this had been apparent to her as she made her difficult journey on the way to adulthood. Inevitably she found herself liking boys and being drawn to them in spite of herself.

She could laugh now at her teenage angst but then it had all been very real. Night after night she'd regularly confessed her deepest thoughts to her diary, writing feverishly on her bed, surrounded by soft toys and posters of boy bands. There was one boy. A tall and unusually calm persona for one so young. Apparently untainted by acne and arrogance, the boy played guitar to himself at break and excelled on the running track. He exhibited none of the 'jock' proclivities associated with sports and yet he was tolerated by the other boys due to his athletic prowess. All the girls worshipped him. There had been a very long line to stand in wait for his attention. She was close to the end of the queue; indeed she believed she was so far back she'd never reach the front. She had been mistaken.

A wretched party had been the venue. Thumping music, too many people and the uneasy combination of school kids and illicit alcohol. Through the gloom she'd glimpsed the object of her adoration in a clinch with a pouting classmate. The envy surged through her like an electrical current. As they fumbled awkwardly in the shadows, consumed by desire and the newness of each other, she'd ached to be in the girls place. Her desire to experience what this girl was enjoying right in front of her eyes was almost a living thing. That was the moment it first happened.

A brief moment of disorientation followed. Later, when she was more used to the sensation, she called it 'the wobble'. She remembered giggling as she'd first confessed it to her diary. A second or so later she looked into the eyes of the object of her affection. She was unalarmed. It seemed so natural. She felt him grope at her buttocks as he pushed his tongue roughly into her mouth. She felt the hairs on his face scratch against her cheek. His breath smelled vaguely of beer which strangely did not repulse her as she felt herself responding to the sheer excitement of the moment. She felt herself kissing him back. That was when she realised all was not as it seemed. She saw a ring on her hand wasn't hers. She saw the blue nail polish she would never have worn. She became aware of breasts were smaller than the ones she prided herself on. She wasn't the instigator of the kiss, she was the experiencer. As the passion of the embrace heightened she became aware that she was somehow a passenger in her classmate's body. Shocked by this realisation, her reaction had been stark fear. In that moment she was once again the observer staring at the frenzied passion in the corner.

As she lay in bed that night she remembered the experience with alarm and excitement. She could still smell him. She shivered as she recalled feeling his erection through his jeans as they'd gyrated together in their exploration. She had never felt so aroused, indeed she still was. She buried her hands between her legs and relived the scenario second by second. When it was over and the flush of arousal had passed she tried to look at the situation logically. She was undamaged; she'd enjoyed the experience, and the two would-be lovers seemed not to have noticed her hitching a ride.

Next day she'd tried it again at school. It didn't work. She found that no matter how hard she tried she couldn't again experience what other people were experiencing. Eventually she'd put it down to alcohol, a claustrophobic smoky environment and a vibrant imagination. That was until she went to stay with her older sister.

If she'd have been born thirty years previously Cassie would have been a flower child. The Hitcher adored her. Ten years her senior, her sister lived in Bohemian splendour in Greenwich Village, writing piercing political pieces on her blog and embracing pretty much everything that life had to offer. Her sister never patronised her. Never treated her as a kid. Always listened to her. Important recognition for a sixteen year old. She'd almost confessed her bizarre story and would have done so had it not been for the arrival of Cassie's latest boyfriend.

Carl was, in her opinion, utterly gorgeous. He made his entrance to the untidy apartment in understated elegance, resplendent in a well-constructed appearance of unkempt affluence. "Hiya, you fucking old fraud," Cassie had laughed at his arrival. Stunned by her sister's greeting, she was even more confused at his chuckling at the outrageous welcome. That evening, as they all ate dinner and drank wine, she began to realise that there was much she had to learn about adult communication. She also realised that Carl was the most beautiful man she'd ever seen. Through the mock shabbiness of his clothes she caught glimpses of a physique that made her almost gawp. His manner, replete with a piercing dark humour, had her hanging on his every word. When he occasionally looked at her it was almost too much to bear.

The evening at an end, she'd helped clear the dishes almost in a dream. She watched enviously as 'Goodnights' were said as her sister and Carl made for the bedroom. While cleaning her teeth, all she could think about was how she wished that she was her sister right now. The 'wobble' followed and, immediately recognising it, she embraced it.

In that moment she was her sister. She lay smiling on the bed as Carl began to disrobe in the half-light. "She's very sweet," he said. "She's going to be a heartbreaker when she grows up." A moment later she was shocked to hear Cassie laugh. "Quit talking about my little sis and take care of business." 'My God', she thought, 'She's actually joking at a time like this.' Carl grinned and removed his shirt. She felt the flush of appreciation as her sister admired the show. She felt her increased heartbeat as her sibling anticipated the moment. When the boyfriend had removed his shorts and had made for the bed she felt her body come to a new height as her sister began to open herself and embrace what was to come. She luxuriated in her sister's longing for the lean hard body. She saw and lived the comfort Cassie felt at seeing his erection, delighted that her body could stimulate such immediate arousal.

In that hour she learned, experienced and eventually understood a level of closeness and intimacy that she could never have dreamed of before: the importance of gentleness and consideration; the stimulation of controlled aggression; the all-enveloping bliss of total surrender to the moment. The musical instrument that was a woman's body that, in the right hands, could be played to perfection by an artiste. The rugged terrain that was a man's body. A realisation that they too could be brought to heights that stripped them of their controlled persona and reduce them to the raw animal that was uncontrolled bliss.

She'd slept well that night.

Only when intimacy beckoned, she learned, could she hitch. And she did, again and again. By the time her seven-day break in New York was over she knew her sister and Carl significantly better than she had ever believed possible. She also knew that she had to have what they had. Regular and quality sex. She was too immature to notice that she only experienced the emotions linked to sexuality.

Upon her return to school she thrust herself into the melee and within six months had been so disappointed with what the local boys had to offer she'd driven herself half mad with frustration. The unsophisticated fumblings of her peer group almost repulsed her. Even when she hitched to her classmates the results were inevitably the same. She began to despair. As her disappointments continued her frustration grew as her needs went unsatisfied.

Her seventeenth birthday had been the first turning point. A classmate's vacationing parents had made the inevitable mistake of letting their son arrange a party during their absence. A senior boy; she'd managed to gain an invite as a few months previously she'd given him a blow job that had sent him half mad with the quality of her technique. It was her sister's star turn. Sadly his own ministrations were both inadequate and frankly embarrassing. Hoping for a re run he'd urged her to come over. For the first two hours she managed to fend off his unwelcome advances then, as midnight approached, she'd made for the bathroom upstairs. Walking down the long hallway she saw one of the senior girls, a lissom Barbie look alike, knocking on one of the bedroom doors. The Hitcher, for reasons unknown to her, stopped in her tracks and watched. "Open up lover," hissed the girl. "It's me." The door opened and the girl slipped in. Instinctively the Hitcher concentrated, embraced the wobble and, a moment later, felt herself inside the secretive doorknocker. It was dark in the room but the Hitcher hardly noticed. She was too intent in trying to come to terms with the feelings of her subject. Unabated rampaging arousal. She watched through the girl's eyes as she feverishly locked the door behind her, almost manic with excitement.

As the girl turned, the Hitcher was aware of her shortness of breath. The girl was on fire. Her subject roughly embraced the occupant of the room, running her hands though long cascading hair and pressed her mouth on soft lips. The Hitcher's mind reeled. She heard a giggle and felt her hands pushing up a micro skirt and under a thong. One part of her almost rebelled, but the other part was caught up with the passion. She felt a slim, long nailed hand press urgently between her own legs and was shocked to feel she was soaked. Moments later she felt a deliciousness as the girl's lover hitched up the Barbie clone's t-shirt and grabbed her breasts, squeezing, exploring. As she felt a moist tongue on her nipple the Hitcher thought she'd explode with the intensity of the feelings. She could literally smell the object of Barbie's attraction. A strong scent that demanded exploration. She felt light headed as she ripped off the girl's thong. She plunged her head between the perfect legs and tasted her.

That night the Hitcher learned two things. Her hitching options had now multiplied significantly, and sex between women wasn't always the soft focus nonsense portrayed in art-house movies. It could be hard, aggressive and demanding. She liked it. No, she adored it.

As the months progressed, she learned to pick her subjects carefully. By the time she'd reached eighteen she was a veteran. By frequenting the right bars and clubs she learned to select the objects of her interest with skill and precision. She hitched and enjoyed the most perfect of men and the most beautiful of women and sometimes, to her utter delight, both at the same time. She hardly bothered trying to do it for real as her own experiences paled into insignificance when compared to those that came with her gift. She all but gave up trying. 'Why bother?' she thought.

By twenty-one she considered herself a connoisseur of the erotic. In her search for the ultimate rush her exploration widened and she took to stalking those who she felt were sufficiently hedonistic to provide her with the stimulation to satisfy her need for a bigger hit. She gave herself over to the eclectic, the exotic and the bizarre.

One evening, as she stood naked in a dark room with her arms bound above her, enduring the lash of a masked man's bullwhip, a thought occurred to her. She felt her subject twist as the leather resounded on her back and briefly savoured the feelings of subjugation and submission and the release that they promised. As the whip fell again she arched her back and savoured the fine line between pain and pleasure. She was in too deep to realise that she was all but lost in her search for the ultimate experience of sensuality. As the whipping continued she was torn between her new thought and the possibilities it offered and the deliciousness of her total abandon to the man abusing her. The pain of her predicament focussed her thoughts but the arousal of her 'Hitchee' confused them. She tried to concentrate on the thought process whilst part of her savoured the submission of her subject. One more stroke was enough. It was time for an experiment. She jumped out.

She sat in a large hotel lobby and watched couples collecting their keys at reception, returning from dinner and nights out. She studied each couple carefully until she found what she wanted. It didn't take her long. She rarely made mistakes. Her selection made, she initiated her experiment and hitched.

It was different. Incredibly different. Thrillingly different. She felt her muscular arms enveloping the woman. She felt the woman's hand glide to her crotch as the embrace built in passion. She felt her erection press uncomfortably against her shorts. She marvelled in the sheer difference of a man's experience of closeness. She revelled in his awestruck appreciation of the girl's body. The power flowing through the man's body threatened to overwhelm her. She felt the soft moist ring of the girl's mouth close over his penis. So this was why they liked it so much. Their whole sexual experience was so much more localised than a woman's. She felt the man trying to keep control, not letting the moment take him too high. And there it was. She'd never even thought about it before. He was saving himself. His thought process was an amazing mixture. A controlled abandonment to the sensation, an appreciation as to who was performing the act on him and an awareness that after it was over he would need to perform.

She embraced his adoration of the object of his affection, losing herself in his reverie. His incredulity at the softness of a woman's body. His childlike wonder at the sensation of smelling her tousled hair. His delight at her evident appreciation of his body. And then came the moment. Her subject pushed the woman gently back and entered her. The rush. He/she was actually inside her. He/she could feel her...from the inside. The woman had given her lover the ultimate sacrifice. She'd allowed him inside her body.

As the man started to make love she marvelled at the complex thought processes he was experiencing. The sheer bliss of the moment, the delight that his ministrations were being enjoyed and the sublime pleasure of the friction on his penis. When his climax eventually came she was already hooked. The power of the explosion shook her with its power and its focus. The male orgasm was so irrevocably different than anything she could have ever imagined. And, the moment it was over, a sense of exhaustion. The release seemingly draining the man. She immediately understood what she had found so hard to comprehend in the past. Once spent, the sexual urge dropped dramatically. Intimacy remained but the vibrancy and urgency faded, the need for recuperation foremost.

After that she altered her hitching dramatically. She plunged with abandon into both male and female subjects, and when she physically slept with non hitching partners the quality of her performance ensured that she was pursued relentlessly. A tiresome side effect. Though jaded, she continued her search. There was still more. A bigger high. She knew it and consequently her commitment to her addiction knew no bounds.

The nadir came on a business trip. As she nursed a drink in a hotel bar a tolerably handsome man had engaged her in conversation. She endured the exchange through amusement more than anything else. Despite her offhanded responses to his questions the man persisted. As he made his ill-disguised pitch an idea formed in her mind. A new slant that, incredibly, she'd never considered before. She practically force marched him to her hotel room.

As he was about to enter her she hitched and experienced him entering her. She watched herself savour the pleasure she was giving herself. He seemed to know her body better than she did. Every nuance of her eclectic needs were addressed. She watched herself in throes of ecstasy and lost herself in his delight at her abandonment. He was satisfying her, really satisfying her. Though she couldn't feel it she could see her own reactions. Her bell was not just ringing, it was sounding relentlessly out of control. Her subject knew this and savoured every moment. She sank herself into his enjoyment. She was a passenger on her own train to paradise.

As the lovemaking intensified she let every fibre of her being connect with his enjoyment of her passion. This was intensity beyond belief. It was what she had been seeking. She basked in his pleasure at her responses and his own sensations. She marvelled at his seemingly encyclopaedic knowledge of the location of every button she had. As she came close to the moment she made a decision. Seconds before her climax she dropped back into her body to experience what she knew was to come. And then it came. The orgasm that had been building deep within her. The first waves made her dizzy. Wave upon ever increasing wave flowed inexorably from between her legs to the extremities of her body. The final tsunami ripped through her with an intensity that threatened sensory overload. As her body convulsed she was aware that even her fingertips tingled.

When it was over she lay in his arms totally overcome and satisfied. "That was incredible," she confessed. Her partner gently caressed her hair. "It was," he admitted. "Jesus, even your fingertips tingled."

She pulled back from him in shock. He smiled at her. "What?" he said. "Did you think you were the only one who could do it?"

- The End -

ALIENS

The exobiologist scratched her head as she tried yet again to asses her findings. Her report was way overdue and she was concerned, she had a reputation to maintain. She stared out of the window in frustration at the enigma that were the inhabitants of the planet below. The captain's table awaited and he didn't like to be kept waiting. After all, it was her job to study new races and report her expert findings, a role in which she normally excelled. Her input was vital; indeed no contact would be made with an alien species until it had been assessed that there was benefit to both sides. Too many mistakes had been made in the past and valuable resources wasted.

She studied her findings yet again. Firstly, they were extremely fragile as they were almost totally composed of liquid. It was frankly amazing that they held together at all. Incredibly, they also had to constantly absorb gas to survive. Their method of communication was extremely unusual. It comprised of vibrating various body parts to create an atmospheric based harmonic which could apparently be registered and interpreted by other members of the race. It had taken an inordinately large amount of computer time to decipher these harmonics and construct a model of what they used as a language.

It was the language model that had caused her the most difficulty. At first it was seemingly incomprehensible. It was only her enormous experience and the powerful mainframe on the ship which had enabled her to painstakingly put together a highly complex algorithm that had finally made interpretation possible. That was when her real problems began.

The captain gently chided her on her lack of progress. "It's most frustrating I must admit," she said as she enjoyed her meal. "Not only is their method of communication bizarre, and believe me I've seen a few unusual races, but it's formalised to a degree beyond imagination. They have an enormously complex protocol involved in social interaction. It's not even true communication as we understand it, it's more like giving hints to whomsoever you're communicating with and letting them join the dots. They use a vast range of highly refined visual and vocal structures which are designed to disguise what they're really saying. How they impart information to others of their race seems to be more important than the actual information itself. To communicate what you really mean seems to be impossible, indeed it appears to be culturally unacceptable. How they actually developed technology is a mystery. And don't get me started on their mating rituals; I'm amazed they actually procreate at all. God knows why they even bother."

The captain smiled. "I think I've heard enough, Doctor." He touched a pad on the table. "Bridge, we'll leave orbit immediately and continue on our way."

The ship slowly manoeuvred a safe distance from the Earth and initiated the Star Drive.

- The End -

WARRIOR

At the priest's instruction the congregation knelt and prayed. Somewhat stiffly the Major followed suit. Three rows behind him a woman nudged her husband sharply in the ribs and hissed, "There's something I never thought I'd live to see." Her long-suffering spouse regarded the object of her observations and blinked in amazement. The general had been in the military long enough to know of the uneasy relationships his charges had with the Almighty, but to see the major in this place was something that he could have never predicted. The priest also glanced uneasily over the rim of his half moon spectacles, noticing the Major for the first time and shivered. He regarded himself as a force for good. He knew that the soldier now bent at prayer had vanquished more evil than he ever would, but the man scared him.

The major was the most outstanding individual under the general's command; indeed he was one of the most highly regarded and well-decorated servicemen in the entire armed forces. In this age of high tech weapons when it was fashionable to look less admiringly at that highly trained and able group of men known as 'special forces', the major was a legend. A consummate commander and a veteran of Panama, Grenada, Iraq, Afghanistan and numerous 'black 'ops' under contract to the CIA.

His achievements and exploits were legendary amongst those with the security clearances to know his work. The major was an enigma and a solid gold asset. Possessed of a loving wife and two delightful daughters, he was famed as a family man beyond repute, but the enemies of the state saw a very different side. The general knew him to be a totally ruthless cold-blooded killer. The jungles of Central America and the backstreets of the Middle East were the theatres where he plied his deadly trade. Many a warlord or drug baron had quietly vanished after having been tagged for the major's personal attention.

His reports made for chilling reading, as did his methods. You didn't assign the major to a task, you unleashed him. Whether it be assassination or a full-blown military engagement, the man delivered. It was only his acerbic and blunt manner that had kept him from higher office. The general was aware that the major had the intellect to appreciate this. The general also knew that the major was doing what he did best…he was a soldier…plain and simple.

The major felt the general wife's eyes on his back and his keen hearing heard her words perfectly. Not ten days ago that hearing had proved very useful in a Sudanese slum. There were three empty spaces at the mosque the following day as a result. Africa beckoned next. A particularly brutal dictator was living on borrowed time. From the moment the major had received his assignment the despot's days had been numbered.

It was not of his mission that the soldier thought now. He'd come to this place as a last resort. He wasn't a God fearing man. He feared nothing. He'd come as a result of a nagging pain in his chest. The men in white coats had told him that he had a year at most. He certainly wasn't afraid of dying, but he was afraid for his family afterwards. He knew he could protect them against anything while alive, but he of all people knew what the world was like. He had been assured that this was one battle that he could not win, and the bleakness of leaving those he truly loved was intolerable. He'd begun to quietly make the arrangements necessary for the dark days ahead and had concluded that his love for his family demanded he try every option to keep them safe. And so he prayed for them. He prayed that for them after he was gone. He felt no awkwardness at being in this place; for him it was a matter of covering every base, no matter how extreme.

So massive was the heart attack that struck him he didn't have time to even register the pain as he pitched forward in his pew.

He'd never learned to ride a horse and yet he was riding one now. The soldier thundered across a grassy veldt under an impossibly beautiful blue sky. The wind tore through his hair and made his eyes water as his powerful mount made short work of the undulating land. He was aware that he had never felt so alive. He breathed in deeply, the smell of the rich earth and the scent of flora around him filling his head.

He sat in silence as the magnificent animal beneath him came to a halt and caught its breath. He unbuttoned his dress tunic and considered his position. A moment ago he'd been in church. Now he was riding a horse in the middle of nowhere. He couldn't ride a horse. Before he had a chance to think any further he saw a figure walking towards him. It was a man, tall and proud. 'No,' he thought, 'not proud, confident.' As the stranger walked towards him his training took over. Physically the man was no threat; indeed few men were to the major. Dressed in jeans and t-shirt, he was apparently unarmed, another plus, though where he had come from was impossible to tell. One moment the major had been alone in this place, this beautiful place, and the next minute the man had been walking towards him.

The man called out to him, "So you made it then?"

The major shook his head and tried to clear his thoughts, but found to his surprise that they were crystal clear. He was alive, deliciously and wonderfully alive. He thought of his wife and daughters in an almost abstract way. His love for them was there, undiminished and vibrant, yet it seemed to be somehow 'managed'. It was almost as if his brain had parked them in a file to allow him to think of other things. He knew that moments ago he had been in church and now he was here. He knew this to be an impossibility and yet this process also seemed to have been 'parked' somewhere in his psyche. It was as he considered these weighty matters that the man finally reached him and spoke. "Don't try to work it out," he said. "We'll have plenty of time to talk about it. Just enjoy the view."

And what a view it was. In the distance, snow tipped mountains capped the horizon. The land was lush and the air was as fresh as he'd ever known. A dense forest covered the land to his left, and to his right a fast running stream made its way urgently to who knew where. The whole place seemed to pulsate as if alive. He actually 'felt' as if he was part of the vista before him. It was almost as if he was the land and the land was him. The feeling was so familiar. He searched for the words. "Harmony," said the stranger. "That's the word you're looking for. It's very easy to forget what it's like; most people do."

The major dismounted and regarded the stranger. Before he had a chance to speak the man held out his hand. "Hi," he said. "Welcome to this place...I'm...well...we'll come to that. Shall I call you Major?" The soldier shrugged. "Everyone else does." They shook hands and regarded each other for a full five seconds before they both tried to speak at the same time. The man laughed. "After you," he said.

As he was about to speak the major remembered his heart attack. He suddenly felt sick and disoriented. Immediately the man was there holding him. "Don't worry, it'll pass," he said. As the man embraced him the major felt a wave of compassion pass though him from his touch. It reached every fibre of his being. It was stronger than anything he had ever known; it was beyond tenderness. It was as if every loving feeling that he had ever felt in his life was just the merest sample of what was to come. He felt himself dissolving into it...dissolving into a place where there was only that feeling. It was only with the greatest of efforts that he pulled himself back out of it and stood up abruptly.

The man smiled at him. "They said you were strong," he laughed, "I'm glad." Trying to gain some sort of equilibrium, the soldier took a deep breath. "I think I died but I don't feel dead. In fact I feel more alive than I've ever felt. I miss my family and yet I seem to be dealing with it in a way that I can't describe."

"I know," said the man, "Everything will be explained soon. Trust me."

The next thing that the major knew, he and the man were on horseback side-by-side trotting gently toward the undulating horizon. The soldier asked the inevitable question. "So where is this place and why am I here?"

The man thought on this for a moment. "You are here because your help is requested. Here, of course, is Heaven." The major stopped his horse. "Heaven? I don't believe in Heaven!" "I know," the man replied, "But a very small part of you does and always has. You've always believed that if there was a Heaven it would look like this. That in itself is a form of belief…and …well…here it is…I think it's rather nice."

He started his horse moving again and the soldier followed suit. "If this is heaven then I…I," His companion laughed. "You thought that if there was a heaven and a hell then it was a difficult call for someone to make because you're a killer. Well, you're right; it was a difficult judgement call. There are those who would call you a murderer and those that would call you a warrior. You killed for what you believed was right. You felt that you were good fighting against evil."

"I was fighting evil," snapped the soldier,

"Tell that to the children of a third world warlord whose throat you've cut," replied the man. "Look," he continued, "I'm not judging you, I know all the political arguments and I know you believed you were doing the right thing. Don't worry about that for now." He suddenly pulled up his horse and the Major did the same.

The man fixed him with a look that the major couldn't fathom. Nervousness maybe? A hint of fear? "You're afraid," said the Major. It was a statement. "What are you afraid of?"

His companion considered his reply carefully. "My name is Arbatel," he said." My function is to reveal why you are here. The reason you are here is over the next ridge. Please do not speak further until I tell you. I need to have all my awareness focused on our safety." With that he nudged his mount who started to move slowly forwards. The major followed him.

As they reached the top of the ridge the sky ahead of them darkened and the lush vegetation began to thin out. As they continued the sun dimmed further and the ground became blackened, as if a forest fire had recently torched the land. Finally they stopped.

"This is the very edge of Heaven," Arbatel whispered. "This is where good and evil meet. Not far from here, dark forces are mustering their armies. This is a place where the good must be very cautious. There are depraved spirits here whoring for souls."

"Hell?" exclaimed the major.

Arbatel held his finger up to his lips. "Quiet. There is great danger here." Suddenly the ground shook violently. The major's horse reared up, throwing him to the ground. As he tried to get to his feet he saw the earth split open in front of him, the tear venting incredible heat. He held his hands up to his face to protect himself. As he did so he felt something hit him hard and fast. Winded, he fell back to the ground. In that moment his experience took over. He rolled over twice concentrating not on his assailant but on getting his breath back. By the time he'd rolled the second time he was virtually recovered. He saw a flash of metal and heard an unearthly shriek. Instinctively he came up, lethally fast. His fist, hard as a rock, connected with flesh. A moment later he was on his feet. His opponent was rolling in the dust, clutching his chest in pain. The major hesitated for only a moment as he registered what had attacked him. A second later he fell on the demon, using the full weight of his body to drive his elbow into its throat. Only when the twitching stopped did he ease the pressure.

A scream of fury behind him made him turn his head. In that moment Arbatel leapt between the major and the charging demon. A brilliant light surrounded the major's companion. He thrust his arms wide and the t-shirted, denim clad guide was no more. In his place, with magnificent wings fully extended, stood an angel. "Be gone," he shouted. Stopping dead in its tracks the monster cowered down, spitting venom at the apparition before him. Arbatel took a step forwards and the demon turned tail and ran.

The major looked down at his slain adversary. It was the most obscene thing he'd ever seen. Humanoid, yet squat and heavily muscled, the naked beast lay twisted on the scorched ground. The demon's yellow eyes stared back at his killer seemingly watching him even in death. Arbatel's voice startled him. "Don't get eye contact. Even in death these creatures are dangerous." He stepped in front of the soldier, blocking his view. The major could have sworn he was taller. Naked, save for a brilliant white loincloth, Arbatel stared intently at his companion and folded his wings behind him. Incredibly, the major laughed. "Yep, you're a real angel all right. No doubt about that."

Arbatel gave him a look that was unfathomable. "You're just like I imagined an angel would look," the major continued.

"I know," the man said and started to walk back to his mount. The Major followed.

"The reason I'm in Heaven,' the major said. "You said it was in this place. Was this what it was all about? I don't understand."

The Angel shook his head and turned around, "No Major. This was just a sample. You see there's a war in Heaven."

The soldier's vision wavered slightly. He blinked to clear his sight. He was in a smoky bar, busy with people. He blinked again and shook his head. The smoky bar was still there. A jukebox blared out country and western music while red-necked men drank in the low light. Instantly on his guard, the Major assessed in a heartbeat that there was no one in the bar who could physically challenge him. Unsure what to do next, he noticed the barman making eye contact and waving him over. He pushed his way through a sea of denim and checked shirts until he reached the bar. The heavily tattooed barman deposited a beer in front of him. "On the house Major, good to see you buddy."

Nonplussed, the soldier picked up the drink and nodded thanks. "You know me?"

"Of course. Everyone here knows you. Look around," the barman urged. Looking slowly around the room the major acknowledged familiar nods from a number of the drinkers.

"There's someone here who wants to see you," the barman continued. He indicated a man in a sweaty white vest downing a shot of tequila in the corner. As he replaced his glass on the table, the man lit a cigarette, inhaled deeply, then poured himself another shot from a bottle on the table. "He looks busy to me right now," observed the soldier.

The barman laughed, "He's got things on his mind. Trust me, he asked for you."

Taking the direct approach, the major pulled up a chair next to the smoker. The man looked up. "Slammer?" he asked.

Ignoring the offer the soldier cut to the chase. "And this is Heaven too? I don't think so."

Downing another shot, the man laughed and then coughed uncontrollably on his cigarette smoke. "You'd be surprised," he said. "I recall that in your younger days you felt that places like these were paradise after some of your little adventures."

The truth of his words stopped the major in his tracks. "You have me at a disadvantage," he said carefully.

"I know," was the reply. "I have everyone at a disadvantage. It goes with the territory. Anyway, welcome." He held out his hand. The soldier took it and regarded the man. Early fifties he guessed, the unkempt shoulder length hair making it difficult to asses his age. A striking grey handlebar moustache yellowed by nicotine served to make the task even more difficult. Overweight, sweaty and reeking with body odour, the drinker made for an unappealing vision.

"As you've been told, there's a war in Heaven. I'd value your help." The mans words were delivered slowly and precisely. Not a man normally given to humour, the Major was surprised to find himself laughing for the second time that day. "So I've been told, by an angel actually. He called himself Arbatel."

"Forgive me," said the man. "You must think me rude. I assumed the barman would have told you. I'm God."

The major stood up and breathed in deeply. The calmness that had been his companion throughout most of this day evaporated. He felt rage welling up inside him despite his iron will and self control. "Bullshit," he screamed and brought his fists down violently on the table. "I've played this game as asked. I don't understand what's happened to me. I don't understand why I don't miss my family. I don't know where I am. I met an angel today for chrissakes. I fought a monster. A real live monster." He looked up at the ceiling. "What is happening to me?"

"If you're looking up to Heaven for answers, you don't need to," offered the drinker. "You're already here." With that the major spun around and grabbed the man roughly out of his seat. Kicking the table over, the soldier pushed the man against the wall. "Answers," he demanded. "I want them now." Seemingly unaffected by the chokehold the major had applied the man grinned through his drooping moustache. "I think it would help to have a change of perspective," he whispered.

The major's vision distorted. There was an explosion of light so bright he was momentarily blinded. He carefully took his hands away from his eyes and gawped at what he saw. The man he'd just been pinning against the wall smiled at him. "I clean up well, don't I?" he laughed, "Is this more in line with your expectations?"

It was all there. He sat atop a magnificent raised golden throne, bathed in light, dressed in a cascading white gown that shimmered with iridescence. A pristine white beard reached almost to his waist, matched in colour by the shock of hair reaching down his back. He seemed to have aged immeasurably. A haunting yet beautiful music echoed gently through the marble pillared room. Everything was white save for exquisite paintings that lined the walls depicting Biblical scenes. Seeing his guest was temporarily struck dumb, the man stood up. He threw open a spectacular double door and walked through it onto a balcony. "Join me," he said, "I think you'll enjoy the view."

As if in a dream, the major stepped out and joined his host. He stared at the perfect sky, so blue it almost hurt. He marvelled at the buildings below adorned with flowers, as if each edifice was a celebration in itself. He watched the sunlight reflecting off the myriad water features as if each flicker was actually alive. He saw laughing people, surrounded by soft light, promenading down streets bordered by fantastic statues. Beyond the city a mighty ocean stretched as far as the eye could see.

Clearing his throat the major spoke, "You'll understand I have some questions?"

The man who called himself God laughed. "I'd be awfully surprised if you didn't. Don't worry; I've cleared my diary. Take all the time you need."

"If this really is Heaven, what about where I was riding today, and the bar?"

"Heaven is not what I want it to be, it's what *you* want it to be. What you've seen today conforms to the various ideas as to what you've thought Heaven was in the past. I help you see what you want to see"

"Am I dead?"

"Not quite, but it doesn't look very good."

"You've got a lot to answer for you know, if you really are God."

"Yes, I'm often told that. Are you going to give me the tired old line about mankind being in a mess and the shitstorm that's going on down there? Let's clear that up for starters. I don't make life the crap some people think it is. You do. Everything that's going on down there man created. Lying, cheating, violence, evil, suffering, fear, poverty. Look at you. You're intelligent. You show a tenderness to your family that makes me proud and yet you're a killer." He held his hand up as the major was about to speak. "Yes, I know you think you're doing the right thing and that's the tragedy. The tragedy for mankind."

"Whoa, hold on," interrupted the major. "I kill to protect people. I dispose of those who would do us harm. If they didn't exist I wouldn't have to be a killer. I don't enjoy what I do."

"Don't you?" his host snapped back. "You forget Major, I know you. There is an excitement as you're near to a kill and the thrill of victory when you succeed. Oh, sure you feel bad about the feeling, but it's there all the same.

I understand of course, you have to feel that way to be good at your job, as you most certainly are. It's the reason you are here." The bearded man fixed him with an icy stare. "You have been brushed by the wings of evil. It's difficult to shake off isn't it? It's the edge I want"

Confused by the remark the major gave him a quizzical look. The man took a step forwards and put his hand on the soldiers shoulder. The major felt the familiar sensation he'd experienced when Arbatel had caught him earlier. He fell into the warm void. "You weren't always this way," murmured the man. "I recall when you first killed. You were nine years old and you shot a sparrow in a tree. As it fell it reminded you of a falling leaf. You were guilty about it for almost a full week."

The soldier fell back, shocked. "I never told anyone that. Jesus…err sorry…but fuck…you really are God aren't you?"

The Almighty gave him a nod. "Glad to have finally convinced you. Maybe now we can get down to business." He gestured to the fabulous view. "All this is at risk. The forces of evil have grown strong. They are making incursions ever more deeply. My warriors are not experienced enough to hold them. Our intelligence tells me that soon they will make an all out onslaught against us. I fear that we will not be able to hold them back. I want your skills as a tactician and I want you to train my people. I think you can give us an edge."

Stunned, the major shot back. "Why don't you just wave your 'Almighty' hand and put an end to all this?"

"Why would I do that?"

"What? Why *wouldn't* you do that? Why not save yourself the grief? Why not save all of us the grief? Unless you can't."

"Are you doubting me?" He held up his hand. "It's really OK if you are. You asked a good question."

"And you're avoiding answering it."

"You believe so? You can ask anything you want."

"Why do you need me here to help you?"

"I don't *need* your help...but I'd appreciate it."

"But if you don't need me why have you asked for my help?"

"Don't you think that fighting for Heaven is a pretty good thing to do?"

"Of course, but if you can do it without my help, what's the point of me being here?"

"Are you saying you don't want to help?"

"You know that's not what I'm saying. I'm saying me being here is pretty pointless if you really don't need me."

"You think fighting for Heaven is pointless?"

"I didn't say that...but me being here is pointless if you can do it without me."

"But why would I want to?"

"What?"

"If people didn't want to fight for heaven...what's the point in it being here?"

"But you're God...you have the ultimate power over stuff. You're supposed to have created everything." The soldier paused. "Which means that you must have created this situation. Shit."

"You're beginning to peel the onion. You know I thought I did a rather good job with those. Aren't they great fried?"

The major walked back inside the room, flopped down on a sumptuous chair and put his head in his hands. "I'm living a bloody metaphor. I don't believe it."

The Almighty stood over him. "Yes you are my friend. Yes it is a shitstorm down there where I plucked you from today. I need to know if it's worth it. Whether redemption is possible. Who better than a flawed hero? A man well versed in both good and evil. I selected you very carefully."

The soldier looked at him bleakly. "The future of mankind rests with me?"

"If we win I've decided everything changes. Everything will be different. I'll take a hands on approach. Get involved. That I promise you." The Almighty's voice was deadly serious.

———

It had been a challenging task, especially as he wasn't used to dealing with ancient weapons. He'd had to call on all the history of warfare he'd ever learned. He lectured legions of immaculate angels on strategy and tactics for the coming confrontation. He showed them the essentials of combat, how to kill without hesitation and not to flinch from the horror, how to take advantage of fear and to show no mercy. He explained to them graphically the need to leave no one alive and how to feed on the glory of the kill.

The time came and the very foundations of Heaven shook to the thunder of battle. At the end the major walked onto the field of combat, well pleased with his men. It had been a triumphant rout of the enemy. Under a vivid crimson sunset he looked dispassionately at the obsceneness of the carpet of slaughtered Demons. He saw rivers of blood flowing through the feathers of dead angel's wings. He smelled victory and it was good.

A slight cough interrupted his reveries. He turned to face God. "Pleased?" he inquired.

"Very," was the short reply.

"Everything's going to be different now," stated the soldier. "You promised."

"Oh, I always keep my promises," God continued. "Everything is most certainly going to be different. You have helped me to a great victory today, a victory that changes everything. My enemies have finally been totally defeated. I'm really most grateful. You didn't have to help but you did. You exercised your free will to my total satisfaction, especially with that vibrant imagination of yours."

The major looked at him, not fully understanding his words.

His host pressed his point. "As I told you, I helped you see want you wanted to see. I hoped it would work and it did. I think it's time for another change of perspective." In that moment, the man with the long white beard shimmered in the major's sight blurring his vision. When his vision cleared the Devil laughed at him. "You thought I was God. Thanks to you, I am now."

- The End -

THE TRUTH GAME

They'd dated twice. Not even proper dates really, more like impromptu rendezvous. Even that had been a struggle. She was just so distant. Aloof, almost, but not quite. She was brilliant, certainly. Her take on the challenges that the company worked on was nothing less than revolutionary. Silicon Valley had more than its fair share of electronics geniuses. He should know; he was one of them. She was aware enough to have ascertained this about him. She knew he studiously tried to avoid 'geekness' but was aware enough to know that if he relaxed for even a moment, he'd forget to wear his contact lenses or cut his hair and start obsessing on obscure electronics conundrums or, even worse, comic books. She guessed he'd been lured away from MIT just in time. Now, when his counterparts were busy writing machine code late into the night or discussing infantile science fiction novels over bottles of inferior wine, she approved of the fact that he frequented the gym and tried to direct his ever-active mind to rest.

She was tall, very tall indeed and she walked with a grace that she knew he'd never seen outside of a Hollywood movie. Nobody knew quite where she had come from. The rumours were that she'd met the president of the research department at some kind of soiree. She had evidently offhandedly offered a solution to one of the company's more obscure technical problems with a leap of logic that had him choking on his bourbon. She was hired on the spot. No questions asked and certainly no references. What she'd contributed in that brief conversation had evidently negated the need for years of research. Watching her work, the geek could believe it.

Her work patterns were odd. No doubt about it. She stared into space a lot. That in itself wasn't unusual in their business. But what was unusual was her work area was uncluttered with notes and trial equations. It seemed she just thought about a problem for a long time then just committed it to writing. That being said, she didn't often come up with anything but when she did, Jesus, it made the rest of the group look like kindergarten students.

She'd noticed him on day one. She noticed the fact that he tried to affect a persona with at least a modicum of personality. In fact he stood head and shoulders above his peer group literally and figuratively. She found him intelligent in his way and certainly the most interesting person in the lab, because at least he tried. In itself said something. Mind you though, even being the most interesting man in the room didn't mean very much to her. They were pretty much all children, but, she had to try and make a life for herself which meant mixing with inferiors. It wasn't their fault of course. She was intelligent enough not to judge them for it.

She'd selected him because she had needs, needs that had gone unsatisfied for far too long. Physically he wasn't in bad shape; intellectually he was the very best of a bad bunch and he was a trier. In her search he was the closest she'd come to what she needed. Of course, she'd have preferred an astronaut but what girl wouldn't? Great minds, cared for bodies and enquiring personalities. She had considered NASA but it was just too difficult to go unnoticed in that rare air. Too many practical thinkers. In Silicon Valley she could just fit in in her way and not make waves and exist as best she could.

Date three was at a restaurant selected in all good conscience by her eager date. She drank the wine offered and tried to ignore the fact it was poison. She even made a valiant attempt to look suitably awed at the fact that the animal flesh she was eating oozed blood as she plunged her fork into the steak. Trying to ignore the havoc the repast was wreaking in her system, she desperately tried to be interested in her date's conversation.

His idle wittering, though well meant, was annoying in the extreme, but she appreciated the laudable attempts he was making. He was totally transparent to her, as were all people. She felt constantly guilty about this yet she was aware she wasn't responsible. Well, not totally responsible.

As he meandered along, in apparent earnestness about his fears about global warming, she saw and felt his compassion and sincerity. She also felt the rest of the mix. His nervousness about whether he was making the right impression, his unsureness about her feelings toward him, his efforts in not speaking too quickly and his amusing efforts to appear worldly. Underlying these tremors on the surface of his persona was a vibrant and powerful lust for her body and a keenly felt intimidation of her looks and intellect. She was surprised by none of this. As long as the quantities of each emotion were in a healthy balance she could deal with them. A small part of her even felt a distant affection.

God, she was an enigma. Hotter than his most ambitious fantasies. He couldn't believe his luck. He felt like a gawky child around her. He *was* a gawky child around her, but she seemed to overlook this. She enjoyed a distant amusement as she read his thoughts. Their conversations were challenging in the extreme, especially where work problems were concerned. She seemed to come at some of these challenges, well, so obliquely. She appeared to pluck bizarre yet revolutionary concepts out of thin air and discuss them as if they were commonplace. He had difficulty just keeping up and he was no slouch. MIT only embraced the best of the best.

She was vague about her roots. She looked almost Indian but she most certainly wasn't. She hadn't even told him where she went to school. It wasn't that she didn't answer; it was just that she seemed able to effortlessly deflect direct questions. Her accent fascinated him. Impossible to place. A precise diction, almost surgeon like its usage of the language. She, however, knew how to get information out of him. He sometimes felt when they spoke that he was being gently interrogated. He didn't care; he was happy just being around her. She felt comforted at his acceptance and submission to the force of her presence. Her unexpected suggestion they finish the evening at his apartment was the last thing he expected. She took a modest pleasure in his surprise and gratitude

Two hours later she relished the fact that he was still marvelling at her body. It was perfect. Unnaturally perfect. She had skin so blemish less he found himself searching for imperfections. There were none. She was toned to an almost unnatural level and soft...oh so very soft. She in turn had ignored his many imperfections and lack of technique, concentrating instead on enjoying his enthusiasm and the long awaited physical release that she craved. She was compassionate enough to understand that he had done his best and it would have to do. At least she'd had a modicum of satisfaction and she was pragmatic enough to be grateful for that.

"Have you ever played the truth game?"

His question surprised her. This had come from nowhere. "What?" she said.

"The truth game," he replied. "You're so damn mysterious. You've avoided answering virtually ever question I've ever asked you about yourself. In the truth game we can ask each other questions but the one caveat is, you have to be totally truthful. It's a difficult game if you play it properly, but it can be fun. And you owe me. You've been holding out."

She felt his excitement at suggesting the game and the sense of daring he felt at having been bold enough to ask. Could he take it? It might be interesting to see his reaction. "OK," she said, with a look he found impossible to fathom, "if you're sure you're up to it."

"I'm up for it," he grinned

"We'll see." She smiled back. "I suppose you want to go first?"

"Got it in one. Where are you from? And remember, only the truth. No avoidance or prevarication." He leaned forward, eager for her reply.

"Madrid," she answered.

"But you're not Spanish, are you?"

"No, I'm not."

"What are you then?" he pressed.

"That's a good question. Are you sure you want the answer?"

"Of course. That's what the game is all about."

She looked at him carefully. "It's interesting that you should call it a game. What am I? You really want to know?"

He laughed nervously. "Hey, it's not a difficult question. I've only just started."

"No," she replied, "it's not a difficult question. But the answer is."

"OK, hit me. I can take it."

She took a deep breath and spoke slowly. "I am nothing you have ever even imagined."

She felt his shock and anger at the answer. She felt his hurt at what he saw as her arrogance. She reached out with her mind and sent tendrils of soothing vibrations into his psyche. She felt his surprise as he experienced the intrusion and noted his pleasure. There was some fear, but she helped him manage it.

He felt his anger subside. He felt her inside his mind; he felt her controlling his alarm. He caught his breath. He felt out of control. Feeling this she reached further in and spoke directly to his mind and calmed him. He heard her voice in his head. Her lips weren't moving.

"This *is* the truth game. This is the real truth game. I am not arrogant. I *am* like nothing that you have ever imagined. I am a telepath and an empath and I am alone. Can you imagine what that's like?"

He sat mesmerised as she continued.

"Where I come from we are all telepaths and empaths. What we are doing now is as normal to me as breathing is for you. Now I am alone. I can feel and hear others, but no one feels or hears me unless I specifically direct my efforts, like I am now. If you came to where I am from you would be regarded as handicapped. In my place we all share our thoughts and emotions. There is only truth. Here is a wasteland. There is no true communication. Can you begin to understand?"

"This is the Madrid in Spain that we're talking about?" he thought. She laughed. Really laughed. She let him feel the pleasure she took from his sardonic comment.

"Yes," she said. "Madrid in Spain. And to answer your inevitable next few questions at once, let me ask you, have you ever had the hypothetical conversation with your colleagues, 'If time travel exists shouldn't we be having visitors from the future?'"

He nodded slowly.

"Well, it's now no longer hypothetical as far as you're concerned. I'm one of them."

"Fuck." His profane thought jarred her and she let him know. "You know I'm telling the truth," she thought. "You can feel it in me."

He sat in front of her like a rabbit caught in car headlights. "How?"

"Time travellers from the future are continually visiting the past. It's strictly regulated of course. In my time we're the first generation of humanity to be able to do this. Only highly trained researchers and historians are allowed to make the trip. 'How' is impossible to explain to you. You'd never understand the physics." She felt his questions coming at her like a tidal wave. "'When' I come from is a very long way in your future. We certainly don't use the Gregorian calendar any more. Suffice to say it's many thousand of years from now. I'm telling you this because I 'missed' the return bus so to speak. There was some sort of glitch and now I'm trapped here. I'm telling you because I think you've got the intellect to take it. In my time the human race has developed physically and intellectually. We share our thoughts and emotions continually. There is no privacy because we don't need it. We've evolved beyond it."

"But not beyond conceit and superiority I see." His thought rocked her. "What?"

His mind exploded into hers. "I'm part of the 'clean up' crew. It always takes a while to identify one of your lot. I have to be sure before I make the approach, hence my cover. You've no idea how many of you so called 'pioneers' have been left behind, messing up the timeline. Luckily time is more robust than you'd imagine, and yet your infantile forays into the past cause problems beyond belief. You saw the thoughts and feelings that I wanted you to see. You have so very much to learn. I'm from your future, your very distant future, and I'm here to take you home until you hopefully all grow up!"

- The End -

PROOF

The interview hadn't been going as planned, in fact she was nowhere near to making the progress she'd hoped or expected. People relied on her to probe and get the facts, a task that normally came to her with the ease of breathing, but not today. She didn't consider herself cruel or unfeeling but she was prepared to be brutal in her search for the truth. She'd made heads of state take moments of pause under the onslaught of her interrogations. At the relatively youthful age of twenty-nine she had not only a huge and devoted readership but also a Pulitzer Prize in her pocket, confirmation that she knew what she was doing.

She hadn't wanted the assignment. She was more used to crossing swords with the likes of Obama or Putin as opposed to this smiling new age charlatan sat in front of her. Despite her protestations, her paper had insisted; this man had acquired millions of devotees in recent years and was clearly a social phenomenon that demanded investigation, and as she was the best, she'd been chosen. She considered this as she toyed with her 'lucky' pendant underneath her blouse as Bob answered one of her more acerbic questions.

"This suite?" laughed the man gesturing around. "Actually your paper booked and paid for it. It's rather nice isn't it? A bit gauche for my taste but, I've got to admit...the room service is rather good. Can I get you anything?"

She regarded him bleakly, aware that another of her questions designed to expose this man had failed. The paper could have told her, she thought bitterly. Still, as the true professional that she was, she pressed on. "You don't look very much like a guru to me," she snapped.

"I never said I was," her subject responded.

"You've sold several million books telling people how they should live their lives and how they should think," she snapped. "How can you know what's best for people?"

Bobs smile didn't move. "Have you read my books?" he asked quietly. As quick as a flash she responded. "Of course, I do my research."

"Then you'll know," Bob continued, "I don't 'tell' anyone anything; I merely make suggestions that people are free to acknowledge or ignore. It's all about free will you see. My objective is to help people to achieve what they really want, and I know what that is."

"Isn't that arrogant presumption?" she pressed.

"Not really," he responded. "It's a very easy thing to know. For example, I know exactly what you want in your life." He let the comment hang in the air. She was too professional to be drawn but Bob was unintimidated by her silence.

"It's so easy," he said, "You want what everyone wants. Happiness."

The simplicity and the truth of his answer momentarily fazed her. Before she had a chance to say anything Bob pressed on. "You see Charlotte... you don't mind if I call you Charlotte do you? You think I'm a fake and I con people out of money. That's why you're here today. You don't care about my work, and that's just fine, but I can't be a fake because I've never claimed to be anything. I've no organisation behind me, no fawning assistants or poorly produced cable TV telethons. I earn my income from the sale of my books, and most of that goes to those with less than me; I just keep enough to live on."

Unimpressed by his well-delivered monologue, she continued her questioning. "That's all very well but your book makes it out to be so easy. You're giving people false hopes about achieving happiness and by trivialising real life. There are no easy fixes, and you're conning money out of the people who buy your books to believe that there are." This time she knew she'd get a reaction and she was right.

Bob burst out laughing. "My God Charlotte, you are angry aren't you? To you life is a very serious business and that's just great. You believe all this crap you see around you is real. You know, the only reality is emotion; the rest of it's just made up. We let it influence the way we feel about stuff. What was it you just said? 'There are no quick fixes.' You seem very sure. I happen to disagree with you."

"You're an act," Charlotte offered unkindly. "You say you're not a guru, which is simply reverse psychology. You may dress in Gap pants and have a ten buck haircut but there's no difference between you and those overweight Indian swamis with their flowing hair and orange robes. You've created a cult around your lightweight philosophical psychobabble to extract money from the very people who need to keep hold of it."

"Wow, that's quite a speech," He chuckled. "Let's see if I understand this properly. I don't look or dress like a guru...therefore I must be one. OK, that's a novel way of looking at things. I also take money from people who need to keep hold of it. I take it by this you mean that the more money they have the happier they'll be. Am I right?" She nodded her affirmation. "My books cost around twenty bucks," he continued. "Hardly a life or death amount. Money does not and never will bring happiness, and you are most certainly intelligent enough to know that. I admit it can help to ease the way, but it's only a tool as are all things in this place you call reality."

"There you go again," she challenged. "Psychobabble! *'In this place you call reality?'* You're making hot air sound like hard sense."

"Only because you don't understand what I'm saying," he snapped back equally sharply. His tone surprised her. At first she thought she'd pierced his well presented façade, but there was something in his eyes that told her his response was less obviously motivated. He immediately grinned at her. "Didn't expect me to get grouchy did you? Not very guru like is it? Or maybe it's just a double bluff...you know...that reverse psychology you were talking about."

She fingered her lucky pendant again as she considered her response. As she began to formulate her next question, her subject reached over to a table next to him, selected a beer and took a long slug from it. "Yes I drink alcohol but you'll be glad to know I've given up smoking and I do occasionally have sex, though generally I feel it's something best left to experts, don't you?" She couldn't suppress a childish giggle. "You've got a great smile," he said expansively. "With the reputation you've got I thought my balls would be on the carpet by now. I must be fighting my corner quite well."

Unable to resist she smiled back at him. "You're nothing like I expected," she admitted. "But I still think you talk crap."

"I know you do," he replied gently. "But are you open to a few concepts?"

"Why not?" she said. "My readers will be curious."

"And you're not?" he said, with a twinkle in his eye. "Right," he continued. "Where shall I start? Oh yes...reality...that old hot potato. You look at the Earth and the universe as reality. I don't. My experience is that our emotions are reality and the rest of it is just self-created details. A tableau if you like, to play out our games on, games that have got to seem real for them to have any purpose, i.e. to experience the emotions that make us what we are. We've done a very good job of this, there's balance everywhere. For every up there's a down and for every hot there's a cold. You do believe in balance don't you?"

"I'm not sure I know what you mean," she responded carefully.

"For all this to appear real, it has to be balanced. Without hot, cold wouldn't mean anything. Without poor, rich wouldn't mean anything...do you see what I mean? She nodded. "It's even the same with language," he continued. "After all language is just a way of vocalising this manifestation of what you call reality. Every statement someone makes has an opposite... do you agree?"

"Well...I'm not sure what you're getting at," she replied.

"Let me give you an example," he continued. "If I said, 'The cat is black' the opposite is 'The cat is not black,' with me so far?" She gave him a withering look.

"Just testing," he said with a grin. "OK, let's take the comment *Nothing Unreal Exists*. First of all, do you believe this to be a true and accurate statement?

She thought for a moment and replied "Of course."

"Good." he said. "Now give me the opposite.

"In that case," she said, "It would be *Everything unreal exists*."

He laughed at her. "That can't be right. My comment is a truism, but yours isn't, is it? To make it the exact opposite. i.e. to really balance it, it's got to be not only the opposite of what I say but also be a truism, you see?"

"Oh I see," she said. "Err let me think for a moment. OK, then it would be '*Everything real doesn't exist*'. Oh...now...wait a minute...that doesn't make sense. That's not a truism either. Hold on...let me think about this. Hold on, it's got to be just *Nothing Real Exists*. No that's doesn't work either."

"It's an interesting conundrum, isn't it? It doesn't make sense, unless you look at what the definition of 'real' actually is. If you look at both statements they're saying nothing real *or* unreal actually exists. It's a paradox or what I call a signpost," He said with satisfaction.

"A signpost?" she said with some confusion.

"Yes," he continued. "I know that at another level we actually know we've created all this and we've left ourselves little signposts along the way to show us that it can't be real and to show ourselves the way home. Look at pi for example. It recurs indefinitely so it's an infinitely big number at yet in terms of size it's quantifiable. It shouldn't happen but it does. Another paradox. The universe is replete with examples; I could go on all afternoon."

"Look, this is fascinating dinner table conversation but where does it take us?" Charlotte blurted out with some frustration, "Because of a linguistic quirk and a mathematical anomaly I'm supposed to believe in your stories?"

He laughed again that wonderful rich deep laugh of his, "Of course not, but I wanted to see if you'd take the bait."

"What bait? She asked.

"If you need to ask that then this conversation has been a waste of time," he replied with mock solemness.

"OK OK," she came back, "I'm intrigued…but what now? I…I mean my readers, need more to even start believing."

"Believing?" he said distractedly. "Oh no, that would never do. You've got to 'know' not just to 'believe'. The very word 'belief' implies the possibility of whatever it is not being true. You've got to 'know' before you're able to convince other people."

"But to know what Bob?" she responded, agitated. "What is it you're trying to tell people?"

"That they are capable of anything," he replied. "That they control their world and not the other way around. That they have the solutions to the life events they call problems. That their happiness depends not on the events and circumstances of their life but the way they relate to those self created phantoms."

"And this is your fundamental belief is it?" Charlotte replied, trying to keep an edge of sarcasm out of her voice.

"No, not at all, it's not belief," he chuckled, "I know; I've seen it; I talk with empirical knowledge. I wouldn't be this arrogant otherwise. To do what I do you've got to 'know' not just 'believe.'"

"So what do you know? What have you experienced that we haven't?" pressed the Pulitzer Prize winner, aware that there was a real story now developing. "How can you prove it?"

Bob took a deep breath. "You want proof? Proof that all that we see is an illusion? The Earth, the universe, time and space?"

"It would make a hell of an article," she admitted. "Are you going to show me a miracle?"

"I'm going to show you something that you would call a miracle, but once you understand it you'll see it's not a miracle but a completely natural event. Do you want me to do this? He murmured. She was surprised at the depth of his sincerity.

"Of course," she replied. "I'm a journalist. I seek out the truth. Do your worst"

"Actually," he said brightly. "I'll try to do my best. Show me that pendant you've been fiddling around with." Surprised that he'd noticed, she reached behind her neck, unclipped it and pulled it from beneath her blouse and handed it to him.

He held it in the palm of his hand and considered it intensely for almost a full minute. "You know I gave this to you," he said finally.

"What?" she replied. "What are you talking about?"

"I gave this to you. It was your eighth birthday and you were in Disney World in Florida with your parents. You tripped and grazed your knee. You were crying and your parents were trying to console you, when a man came over dressed in an orange robe. You thought he looked really strange because he had long black hair but a white bushy beard. He asked your parents if everything was all right and when they told him it was, he reached into his robe and pulled out this pendant and told you. "This is a special pendant for birthday girls who are brave enough to stop crying when they've hurt themselves. If you keep it with you it will bring you luck"

She went white and her jaw dropped. "How the hell did you know that? I've never told anyone that."

With great ceremony Bob got up and went to one of the drawers in the locker next to his bed. He slid the drawer open and pulled out the only three things inside. An orange robe, a longhaired black wig and a false white beard.

Charlotte suddenly felt unwell. "That isn't funny. I don't like being made a fool out of and this is really sick. It couldn't have been you anyway, because you're nowhere near old enough."

"Feel your neck," Bob urged. She did so. The pendant was back there. She felt faint.

Suddenly he was right besides her. "Don't worry Charlotte, it's OK, really it is. This isn't a trick, and deep down inside you know that. You've never told that story to anyone, have you? You parents are both dead so they couldn't have told me. When I took the pendant from you a moment ago I just popped back to Disney World and gave it to you. You were standing close to *Pirates of the Caribbean* at the time weren't you? Of course it's easier for me to remember because I was only just there."

She felt the room spinning. This had to be a huge pre planned trick. Bob couldn't know these things. "How did you get changed so quickly?" she said quietly. He smiled at her. "Time is not how you believe it to be. I changed before I left and changed when I got back in the time you thought you saw me looking at the pendant. It doesn't matter how right now, what does matter is that you've seen a demonstration of what I've been talking about."

Her mind raced; surely she was being made to look stupid…when suddenly it came to her. She pierced his elaborate con with a deftness that caused her spirit to soar. "What you say cannot be true," she said triumphantly. "You're saying I gave you the pendant for you to travel back in time to give it to me, so I could give it to you here in the future again. If that's the case, the pendant has only ever been in yours or my possession."

"Keep going Charlotte," said Bob quietly.

"Therefore" she said, executing her coup de grace "The pendant couldn't exist, if it's always been in yours or my possession then it could have never actually been manufactured, because we got it from each other."

Bobs face relaxed. "You're so right Charlotte, it can't possibly exist, and yet you know that what I've done here is not a trick, your intelligence confirms it can't be. You wanted proof didn't you? Didn't you say it yourself a few minutes ago? *Everything real doesn't exist.* Isn't that what I've been trying to say all afternoon?

His words hit her like an express train. The world, as she had known it, vanished.

Bob laughed. "Welcome back," he said.

- The End -

AMBITION

In a time of war, he mused almost regretfully, she would have been a battleship. Vast, imposing and impossibly magnificent, the awesomeness of the Coalition's mightiest starship came into view. Hanging in orbit above Earth's blue oceans, the *Gilgamesh* patiently awaited her commanding officer. *'All I need is a tall ship and the stars to sail her by.'* The words from an ancient novel came into the commander's mind. Romantic notions perhaps, he thought, but nevertheless fitting. He always savoured the short transport trip to his charge. A brief moment of calm before assuming the heavy mantle of responsibility for this beautiful vessel and it's five hundred crew. He liked to think he had something in common with the Sumerian king after whom this leviathan had been named. It was one of the few conceits he allowed himself. In reality of course he knew it wasn't true. He was an intellectual. To command a starship he had to be; a superior brain was a basic requirement. Nonetheless, despite his consummate cerebral skills, he allowed himself the luxury of the whimsical notion that in another time he would have been a warrior king. Like Gilgamesh, he was a leader of men but a leader in a time of peace. No thrill of victory or conquest rewarded his efforts; instead, the challenges of exploration, cutting edge science and diplomacy were his purview.

For most, the achievement of a star ship command was a heady enough victory for even the most ambitious mind yet he found himself unfulfilled. His IQ demanded stimulation yet his responsibilities provided less as time went by. Ten years previously he'd gained his appointment and been the youngest in history to have such a charge. Then he'd relished the fearsome challenges that came with the responsibility; his skills as a tactician, a scientist and numerous other disciplines that were continually put to the test. Equally he'd enjoyed the status and the power that went with the role. The whispered words 'Starship Commander' upon his arrival at social gatherings, by those who could only dream of such majesty, gave him pleasure. He affected indifference to them and to those who were drawn to his power. He chose his physical pleasures carefully, selecting only the most perfect to share intimacy. He comforted himself that although others were, he was not seduced by his power or intellect; nevertheless he allowed himself to enjoy his gifts.

The ship was *his*. He coveted it above all things. Though he was aware that, increasingly, his intelligence was demanding superior challenges, he could think of nothing greater than his command that would provide an increase in stimulation.

A further problem was his executive officer.

The exec was not only insufferably brilliant, but fifteen years his junior … and ambitious. The commander had no problem with ambitious officers; indeed he was a good enough manager to encourage this trait in the people that reported to him. The trouble was that she was rather better than he had been at her age. He acknowledged this to himself without rancour, it was a simple fact and not to be disputed. She wanted his command and he knew it. She wanted it for the same reasons he'd wanted his own command. He was caught in a trap of his own making. His superiors were well aware of his skills and after ten years of command experience they were keen to use his talents to train others. The better he did his job the more likely he was to loose his ship, and the sharp eyes at the Admiralty had clearly noticed his exec. It was a no win scenario…the march of time was his enemy.

It did not help one bit that he actually despised his exec. It was not that she was aloof, even with him, or that she clearly grasped some problems more quickly than he did…it was her manner. Whilst never less than respectful, he knew that she knew she intimidated him. Cognisant that her cool beauty had no effect on him, she used her quick mind instead and it worked.

The exec glanced sideways at the commander. She didn't dislike him, indeed she felt that there was nothing about him to dislike. As far as she was concerned he was a competent line officer. She understood it wasn't his fault he was less able than her. She held this view not in contempt but in a simplistic logical evaluation of his talent when placed against hers. She regarded the commander as simply an unwelcome obstacle to her ambition. She had been patient, knowing that eventually her swiftness of thought would one day show him to be less capable than her, and the powers that be would make the necessary changes. She *needed* command.

As the transport drew close to its destination the true majesty of the *Gilgamesh* became apparent. The bright sunlight almost fell into its dark contours. It was an engineer's dream made reality, the most advanced starship ever conceived. A creation of unimaginable power, capable of travelling at speeds that were science fiction only a few decades previously.

It was concerning speed that this voyage was tasked. There were those who thought that they could make her go even faster.

Einstein had suggested that the speed of light was the speed limit of the universe. Of course both the commander and the exec had read his ancient writings with some amusement, however in his time his views had been far reaching and brilliant. He'd proved that, essentially, the faster one travels, the greater one's mass becomes. He further proved that at the speed of light ones mass would become infinite and therefore it was the fastest one could travel. Of course, knowing what he thought knew at the time, he was quite correct. He'd only begun to have an inkling of quantum mechanics and the true nature of the universe. The eclectic Swiss patent clerk had influenced many for centuries until it was discovered these so called laws could be side stepped quite easily.

In some ways Einstein had been correct. The speed of light was indeed the speed limit of the universe but only in 'normal' space. The solution was simple. To travel at speed greater than the speed of light all one had to do was to create an envelope of space around the ship 'different' from the nature of normal space thus enabling it to break the light barrier as, protected by the envelope, it was not subject to the laws of normal space. It was a system that worked very well.

There was now a body of thought that suggested this thinking was as archaic as Einstein's had once been and the *Gilgamesh* had been selected to demonstrate this. It was these matters that occupied the commander's thoughts as he walked onto the bridge. He noted with some discomfort the new equipment which had been assembled around the navigator's console. The navigator was making no effort to hide his own disquiet.

The exec noticed the Commanders ill-disguised uneasiness. She knew her captain simply didn't grasp the physics of this new drive. Indeed, how could he?...she could only just grasp it herself in its most basic terms. Nonetheless, this edge would make her reports to the Admiralty more impressive than his. It could be enough to move him 'upstairs'. She amused herself by giving the navigator a piercing look which she knew would affect him on numerous levels. His nervous reaction served to make the moment complete and satisfying.

The thinking behind the new drive was impressive...and radical. In basic terms it considered not only the destination for each voyage but also 'where' this destination actually was. 'Where' it postulated, was a relative term. 'Where' is a term that relates to a three dimensional view of the universe. i.e. There are physical co-ordinates that can be detailed in normal space-time for where one is and where one wants to go. The drive engineers had interrogated this matter further and apparently 'proved' that distance was a function only found in three-dimensional space. If space was regarded as having multiple dimensions, then it was feasible that distance was irrelevant outside the parameters of three-dimensional space.

The engineers demonstrated, via some highly baffling equations, that everything and every place in the universe actually existed in one moment and one place simultaneously. Therefore they had developed a 'drive' that would actually create a quantum causality around the ship enabling it to exist in this multi-dimensional realm therefore being everywhere in the universe 'at once'. In that instant of existing everywhere, the ships sensors, set to recognise the destination that the ship had set itself, would literally, electronically, tell the universe where it wanted to go and therefore 'call up' its destination. As one of the engineers described it patronisingly to the Captain. "We literately 'dial up' a destination and its delivered to us without us actually moving. A bit like phoning for a pizza delivery." A senior engineer had chuckled at the analogy. It was close to being true.

Two days later they tried it for the first time. As the drive was initiated the commander had a vivid daydream. He was in amongst blood dripping slaughter on a distant plain, where bronzed men with swords and gleaming armour hacked each other to pieces in the name of God. The Exec also daydreamed. She dreamed of gazing disdainfully at young men who were intimidated by her power.

In a few seconds they travelled a light year…or rather, as the engineer reminded them…they had called the destination to them. Not very far, a mere eight million million kilometres.

A week later they were ready to try again. This time, after five minutes, they arrived at the spectacular clouds of the Magellan Cluster at the very edge of human exploration. Unaccountably, as the drive was initiated, the commander again fell into a jarringly real daydream. He dreamt vividly of the smell of battle and the glory of his first kill. He'd driven a sword down mercilessly into one the barbarians who had invaded his land. His victim's warm blood had spurted over his body and the taste of it lingered in his mouth. He stood victorious and aware that he had never felt so alive. He snapped himself out of it, shocked at the realness of the dream.

The Exec also daydreamed of walking from the Admiralty office with freshly issued orders in her hand. She enjoyed the hushed whispers behind her as she strode towards the transport terminal to take her to her new command, feeling almost overcome with the effect the power had on her.

The engineers fussed over their equipment and fiercely discussed some undecipherable anomalies on their instrument readings. Yes, they had called up where they wished to go, but it appeared that the ships clocks were at variance to the local time at their destination. They had reached the Cluster at a time in the past. They had unwittingly achieved time travel, a rather unwelcome side effect. 'Where' they were 'now' was actually ten years previous to when they'd set off. There were clearly variables in the drive program that they had not fully considered.

The engineers were confident that they had solved the problem. Time travel, whilst theoretically possible, had never been achieved before or even attempted. They apologised for the inconvenience and assured the commander and the exec they could reverse the situation. The problem had occurred, they suggested, due to the nature of space time itself. Not only did the drive put them 'everywhere' at once it put them 'everytime' at once, a variable that they had not considered. The solution was to 'call out' not only the destination but also the required time as well. They were certain that there could be no other variables involved in the procedure, they just needed to be certain of all the parameters that they electronically called out. There was something odd about this thought process at the back of the execs mind, but she couldn't quite grasp what it was. The engineers initiated the drive.

The newly promoted exec stood at the helm of her ship. She couldn't imagine not having a command. She stood erect and proud as her bridge crew went about their business. It was a role that sat well with her; indeed it defined her. Her time as second in command seemed like a dream.

The sun beat upon the commander's back as he sat on his charger ahead of 100,000 baying troops. In the distance he could see the enemy. Heathen infidels who would be vanquished before the day was out. He drew his sword, threw back his head and bellowed the cry of a warrior. His hordes leapt forward as he charged towards the enemy.

The ship's navigator, who had been thinking wistfully about a Caribbean beach when the drive was initiated, gratefully accepted another Pina Colada and gazed with deep pleasure at the turquoise sea. He enjoyed the feeling of the sand between his toes and propped himself up against a palm tree. The exec walked over to him, stunning and bronzed in her swimsuit. She affectionately planted a kiss on his cheek. He couldn't imagine a life better than this…indeed it was the only one he had ever known.

- The End -

THE FUTURE

Being a futurologist in the year 113,435,501,677 was not the easiest of roles. Mind you, he supposed, being a historian was probably a lot more difficult. 113,435,501,677 plus the odd thousand or so years before the Gregorian calendar was brought into use was a lot to learn. Not that he really cared about such matters as he was concerned with what was possibly going to happen as opposed to what had already happened. Sadly, it was sometimes only by studying the past that gave him the clues as to what might happen. Yes, there were patterns amongst the chaos, but mostly it was chaos. He amused himself in lighter moments by studying the predictions of previous futurologists. He hoped that his own endeavours wouldn't provoke the same reactions in his successors.

Some asked why he became a futurologist. The answer was easy. It was one of the last great unknowns. It's mystery intrigued him. There had been a great deal of worry amongst his ancient predecessors when time travel had become reality. Firstly, as a fascinating experiment, and eventually as a pastime of the bored and jaded. There had been a wringing of hands in his profession as they feared they would be put out of a job. The ancient's lack of understanding of the true nature of time was criminal when regarded now with the benefit of experience and research. Untold millennia ago when the first few brave souls had ventured into the future and back again they amazed with grand stories of what was to come. It took a while for everyone to realise that their stories differed on every trip if they picked the same time and location. All they saw of course was a possible future, a permutation on the infinite possibilities that the future had to offer. At the moment they embarked on their trip, they departed from the linear timeline in which they existed to one that was simply a logical extrapolation from the exact moment they made the jump. Even to jump a mere second later brought a different experience. In that one second, enough had happened in the universe to make the outcome different. The Universe was a pretty big place with lots happening in it.

The size of the cosmos had been a subject of intense debate in early human records and, he presumed, even before that. Now of course, he couldn't think of anyone who hadn't ventured to the ends of the universe. What existed beyond that was also well understood. Nothing. The 'whys' of this perplexing enigma were thankfully not his purview. He was a practical scientist not a metaphysical physicist. There was still conjecture as to what was in existence before the Big Bang but, again, it wasn't his purview.

Interaction with alien species had not had a significant effect on the human race. Though eagerly anticipated, the moment of first contact had been something of non-event. It established two things. The first being the fact that the human race was indeed not alone. The second being that aliens were exactly that…alien. Communication had proved totally impossible and had remained so ever since with every race that had been encountered. Primitive writings romantically describing vast intergalactic empires and even the possibly of wars were embarrassingly wide of the mark. It was a simple fact that once a race had worked out how to exceed the speed of light and travel the vast distances needed to actually explore anything of relevance, they had evolved to a level of civilisation that hadn't just renounced violence and conflict; they had simply forgotten about it.

Thus, on the odd occasion when races encountered each other, they simply politely ignored each other. A Freon breathing silicone-based quadruped had little in common with, say, a bloated bag of sentient gas. And those were the less exotic examples.

That the human race had survived beyond the year 2000 was a miracle. Nevertheless it somehow had. It took a while for their primitive minds to address something which they called 'poverty'. A concept that the futurologist had difficulty in fully understanding, nevertheless it was well documented so he accepted it. There was also something called 'disease' which had him reeling in horror when he studied the records. The thought of such an existence made him shudder. The continual references made to an experience called 'pain' sounded downright unpleasant. He had no idea what it meant, but it certainly didn't sound like something he'd want to endure. Thankfully they'd forgone the need for physical bodies eons ago.

This jump had been the last really significant event in the history of what was called the human race. Of course he didn't remember it. It was before his time. He'd been called into existence by his parents well after that momentous event. They remembered it. They'd lived it. How he envied them. He also respected their bravery. Letting oneself be copied as binary code and downloaded onto a mainframe was a pretty courageous thing to do in those unenlightened times. To actually risk one's existence on a scientific principle was radical, certainly with the archaic technology available then. Nevertheless it was successful. Instant immortality was the first advantage. The ability to experience anything within the range of the processing power of the mainframe was the second. Archaeologists called the experience 'virtual reality'. Actually existing as binary code did away with the virtual bit. Their binary world was real. Naturally science soon did away with the need for hard-wired circuitry and soon progressed to more advanced storage mediums based on zero point energy and dark matter making the experiential possibilities almost limitless.

Eventually, even that became unnecessary. Using the very fabric of the universe as a storage medium, they roamed freely throughout the stars. Some vestiges of their physicality remained though. It seemed to be part of the human condition that they more often than not clustered together as if finding solace in companionship. This appeared to be the one constant in human evolution. Being alone for long periods was not pleasurable. Why, no one had yet fathomed.

And thus they drifted benevolently about the cosmos, observing and experiencing the wonders that it had to offer. Occasionally they came to a halt, unsure of what to do next. In those moments they let the heavens pull them along in its wake until, like a shoal of fish, an individual would have an idea and change direction and everyone else would follow. The reason they followed was why the futurologist did what he did. Boredom had set in. In a blink of an eye they could be anywhere they wished, and after many millions of years they'd been pretty much everywhere of interest. If someone even had a spark of a new idea they'd follow like sheep, eager for diversion. His job was to look into the future and suggest what the next step would be, what they could look forward to. What was going to change? He was a giver of hope. His companions hung on his every word. There had to be something else. Something more. Everything had been the same for so very long.

The two scientists studied their experiment carefully. "Damn," said the more senior individual, "An evolutionary cul de sac. I don't understand it. I was so sure that I'd given this group all the tools they'd need to progress but they've just hit a brick wall."

His colleague smiled. "Don't be so hard on yourself. This area of expertise is a challenge. That's why we chose it, remember? I'll destroy this batch and we'll try a few new tweaks next time out. After all, tomorrow's another day."

- The End -

AN ASTRONAUTS DREAM

The doctors had assured her she wouldn't dream, and in fairness, she hadn't. These were the first thoughts that occurred to the astronaut as she began her slow wake from hibernation. As she felt the robot probes injecting her body with electrolyte solutions and various assorted stimulants to aid her return to consciousness, her training began to take over. 'Cygnus' she thought. 'We're finally there'. Eighty three years lying in this high tech tomb, watched over by the ever present unblinking eyes of the computers monitoring her every body function was at an end; machines that had ensured her very existence as her ship streaked through the hostile vastness of deep space towards her final destination. 'Where none has gone before,' she thought, the enormousness of her situation undulled by the sluggishness of her awakening thought processes.

By now, she mused, braking procedures would have been initiated. Her ship, the mighty *Hector,* would be shedding incalculable kilo joules of energy as the star drive wound down. Within a few days the ship would have stopped completely and her charge would be sat silent, surrounded by sights new to human experience. An end to an epic journey and a fitting achievement for the most advanced spaceship ever created. The *Hector* was a true *Ship of the Line;* the commodore's insignia on her uniform was a testament to this. She allowed herself the luxury of a smile as she considered her achievement.

In twenty-four hours her second in command would awaken and so would her chief engineer to oversee the last stage of their deceleration. As commander it was her privilege to determine that she was awakened first to enjoy a delicious twenty four hours of solitude and experience the sights of deep space so very far from home with no distraction. In a week or so the rest of the crew and the colonists would be woken including her own personal companions. She thought with pleasure and longing about Lara and Tekashi. Both so very different and yet both so appealing and, mercifully, unintimidated by each other. An affectionate triumvirate whose love had grown so fast that it had bewildered her and hopefully would survive the challenges of their brave new worlds.

After a few minutes she felt strong enough to speak, but when she tried all that she could manage was a pathetic squeak. 'Strange,' she thought. 'I should be able to speak almost immediately.' She put it down to an inordinately long time in hibernation. Her previous maximum had been a mere two years. Eighty-three years was bound to be different. Half an hour later she felt almost ready to sit up but she still found she was almost unable to move beyond the odd twitch and, more concerningly, it was still impossible to utter an intelligible sound.

A wash of concern passed over her. Something was wrong. She should be returning to normal far more quickly. She was unable to interface with the main computer as it was voice activated though she knew its systems would be waking her up as carefully and as quickly as possible. She reasoned that the only thing she could do was wait in a state of some anxiety until she was fully revived.

The hours passed inexorably slowly as she waited for the first signs of mobility and speech, a process that should have taken thirty minutes maximum, even after all these years. It was a most shaken Commodore who crawled from her capsule almost a day later. Shakily she stumbled across the floor to a terminal and tapped the 'Interface enable' key. Still unable to speak properly, or most certainly not in a manner where the computer would recognise and respond to her, she keyed in her clearance and enquired

Ship status?

After what seemed like an age an answer appeared on the screen.

Nominal.

Unappeased and annoyed by the brevity of the response she keyed in.

Current velocity and position?

Again a full thirty seconds passed before the reply flashed up on the screen.

Current velocity zero, position unknown.

She blinked in disbelief and rapidly typed

Why is position unknown? When did we stop?

The cursor oscillated briefly then typed out.

Position unknown due to no frame of reference. Ship stopped fourteen hours and fifty-three minutes ago.

Confused, she typed again.

Take position from star fixes.

This time the reply was immediate.

No stars available for fix.

A sensor malfunction. A serious problem at this stage of their mission. She was immediately concerned. She resumed her interface.

Run full diagnostic on sensors.

The computer immediately replied.

Initiated.

As the computer commenced its investigations, she made her way painfully over to one of the windows in the hibernation chamber and hit the button to raise the screen. As the screen went up she looked eagerly to see the star system she had travelled so very far to find. She looked into an inky blackness and could see nothing. She reached out and dimmed the room's lights to get a proper view but it made no difference. It was like looking into pitch-black nothingness. Someone clearing his throat courteously behind her made her jump out of her skin.

"I'm awfully sorry to startle you," said a shadowy figure in the gloom of the darkened room. Reacting immediately, she hit the normal lighting button which revealed a kindly looking elderly man dressed in what looked liked the sort of costume that was difficult to place. Maybe Indian or Srilankan she thought, though the man appeared to be a Caucasian.

She stared at him, knowing she couldn't speak, afraid but unwilling to show it. The man waved his hand gently and said. "It's ok, you can talk now. You should start feeling better shortly. Who am I? Well it's a good and simple question but a long answer I'm afraid."

She spoke, slowly at first getting used to using her voice again, "Computer, intruder alert, initiate all high security protocols. Start waking procedures on security detail."

The old man chuckled. "I'm sorry, but the computer is only operating at its most basic level though, one has to say, considering everything, it's done rather well. I really think we should talk." As he spoke she watched him carefully, trying to evaluate him. He seemed totally at ease yet he had no apparent back up despite his intruder status. The man smiled at her and eased himself into a chair.

"I'm unarmed, benign, unaccompanied and here to try and help," he said. "We've lots to discuss."

"My crew and passengers..." she began to say.

"Are safe in hibernation and unharmed," the man replied, cutting her off. "Let me try to make it a bit easier for you. Let me tell you what I know." She was about to interject, not used to having someone else take the initiative but the man held up his hand and said, "Please indulge me. You set off on your valiant trip to travel a great distance to colonise and terra form new worlds. It was a laudable exercise. Your ship actually had a star drive which was rather clever I must say. There aren't many who worked out how to do this. What was it you called them? Tachyons. Yes that's it, tachyons. What a wonderful name. Yes, they do indeed travel faster than light and your people worked that out. Very clever, very clever indeed."

She made to speak but he silenced her with a look, a slightly more serious look this time and continued. "You can ask whatever you wish…when I've finished." He settled himself more comfortably in his chair and continued. "A few weeks after you set off you initiated the star drive which was programmed to push you towards Cygnus where you would arrive after eighty three years. Despite the fact that the drive was capable of huge velocities, it took many years to accelerate to the speed you thought was possible so you left it to the computers to manage this function and, so to speak, you took to your beds to sleep through what would have been a rather tedious journey. What you don't know is that initially everything went to plan until just after you passed Proixma Centauri. Now, you must understand it wasn't your fault; it wasn't anyone's fault, it's just one of those things that happen. Shortly after Proxima Centauri you had a small encounter, a very small encounter indeed, with a minute particle of space dust that had been rushing across the universe since the dawn of time itself. While you slept, this particle, no more than a micron or so wide, hit your ship and went straight through it. It was so small even the sensors didn't notice the microscopic hole it made in your hull. Alas this particle blasted through your computer core and destroyed a few lines of machine code…a few critical lines unfortunately. It caused what you would call a catastrophic protocol failure. You do like those complex words don't you? The result of this was that the computer forgot to turn off the star drive and, as the deceleration program was linked to your 'wake up' program, this was also forgotten. So you kept accelerating and kept going."

"We're not at Cygnus?" she asked.

"Err, no…I think we can safely say you missed your stop."

"So where are we and who the hell are you and how did you get onto my ship?" she snapped.

Apparently unperturbed by her manner the man answered. "Sadly this where the answers to your questions become a little more, shall we say... enigmatic?"

"Try me," was the terse reply.

"Which question would you like answered first?...actually I'd better answer the first one and then the answers to the second and third question may make slightly more sense," he said. Before she had a chance to say anything he continued.

"Your ship just kept accelerating and accelerating and just kept on going until there was nowhere else to 'keep going' to. Not to put too finer point on it...err how do I say this...you're at the end of pretty much everything actually. Before you ask the next question, which I know will be 'How long have we been asleep?' I must tell you that if I tried to tell you that in that wonderful base ten numbering system that you use I'd still be chattering out zeros in a few days time. Just trust me that's it's longer than you could ever begin to imagine, hence your difficulty in waking up. I must say, your machines did a rather good job keeping you alive."

She was too intelligent to think he may be joking. This was not a colonist who had somehow awakened to play a practical joke. This intruder was either very dangerous or very powerful, or perhaps both.

"Yes, you're right," the man murmured. "I am powerful as far as you're concerned, but most certainly not dangerous." As she was about to speak he again held up his hand to silence her and continued. "And in answer to the third part of your question, which you may recall was, 'who am I?' that is a slightly more difficult one to answer. Forgive me if I save that bit of information until you've asked me a few more questions. I can see you're just bursting with them and understandably so. Don't worry, we've got plenty of time, because here time doesn't exist, at least not in the way you think about it."

She tried to read his expression but found herself unable to. Her first thoughts were about the safety of her crew, passengers and ship. The next priority was the mission status. This strange interlocutor was a command problem that she could have never envisaged. If he was a saboteur why was he bothering to talk to her and what would he be hoping to gain? He clearly wasn't a colonist (he could never have taken himself out of hibernation) and she knew all her crew member's faces and he most certainly wasn't one of them. His story was obviously preposterous, so what was he doing there and what was she going to do about it?

"Just the thoughts one would expect of a quality commander," the old man said, startling her. "Yes I can read your mind; it's frankly a lot easier than using speech. So much less restricting. My story is not preposterous, it's true; your crew and passengers, as I've said, are fine but your mission is compromised by a factor that is way beyond your training, experience or understanding. And, as I know we're going to have to get around to this sooner or later...I am the one who created all this."

"What?" she snapped, "You created these problems?"

"Very indirectly...yes," he replied. "But what I really meant is that I created...well...all of it really." He made a grandiose gesture.

"You're a ship designer?" she said.

He laughed great guffaws until his shoulders shook. "No, no, no," he said, "Not just the ship...everything...what you call the universe actually."

Something inside her snapped. "Let's get this straight. I'm at the end of the universe yes? And I suppose you must be God then? Nice outfit by the way. Call me cynical but piss off and let me check some facts for myself." With that she strode past him into the corridor and made her way to the bridge. As she stamped her way towards an elevator she shouted, "Computer, is voice interface activated?"

"Enabled," came back the pleasant female voice.

"Computer," she continued, "how many years has this mission lasted so far?" By the time she had entered the elevator and subsequently reached the bridge, the computer was still chattering out the trillions of zeros needed to answer her question accurately. "Computer stop" she barked as she walked out onto the bridge. The computer's confirmation of the stranger's affirmation did nothing to ease her mood. "Main view screen" she said as she stood on the command deck. The screens whirred back revealing a 180-degree view outside the ship which showed…nothing…just the same inky blackness she'd seen from the hibernation port. "Computer, how many light years have we travelled?" she asked with some exasperation. Two minutes later the computer was again still chanting the almost infinite number of zeros needed to answer her question when suddenly it went quiet. The stranger was standing next to her.

"That's enough. Time for some empirical experience," he said gently. With that the bulkhead next to them vanished, opening the bridge to deep space. Shocked she stood back. "Don't worry," the old man said. "I'm taking care of your breathing…please follow me," and with that he walked outside.

He stood looking at her, seemingly floating in black nothingness some ten meters outside the hull "Com'on," he beckoned. "What have you got to lose?" Nothing in her training or experience had prepared her for anything like this. Her mind raced trying to rationalise her situation but came up with nothing. The computer had confirmed that she had been asleep for untold millennia and she had travelled a distance that seemed to be unquantifiable in physical terms. Additionally this stranger seemed to know all about it and had the power to read her mind and make walls vanish, powers that revealed not inconsiderable abilities yet mercifully he appeared friendly. She conceded it would probably be best to just play along until the purpose of her situation revealed herself. With that she took a tentative step outside her ship and found it was just like walking on a normal floor. Though she was surrounded by pitch black there was illumination provided by the ship's navigation lights so she was afforded a clear view of the man.

"There," he said. "I told you it would be OK." He pointed to his left and said, "What can you see?" She looked into the blackness and could just make out a smudge of white light. "What do you think that is?" he asked.

"I have no idea." she replied honestly.

"It's the universe." he said, "And it's coming. Or should I say... expanding...our way."

"So where are we?" she responded as quick as a flash.

The man made a slight motion of his hand and two easy chairs appeared. He motioned to one. "Please sit." So she sat. She sat on an easy chair suspended apparently in thin air and contemplated the vastness of her ship, the stranger and the pale smudge of light that was supposedly the universe. She thought. She thought like she'd never thought before; she thought until her head hurt and finally came to a conclusion then spoke, slowly and carefully. "If what you and the computer say is true, we've reached the edge of the universe and passed through it. Physics dictates that where nothing happens or no events occur there is nothingness. My ship has passed beyond the event that is the universe and by doing that has created an 'event' outside the universe hence me and my ship being here has called this place into existence."

"Bang on!" said the man with some enthusiasm. "Very good...very good indeed." She was childishly pleased with the man's patronising ebullience but she tried to shake off the feeling and keep her thought processes logical.

"And you say you created the universe?" she said, trying not to sound sarcastic.

"I most certainly did but despite what you said earlier I'm not suggesting I'm God, or at least not in the way you would think about that entity." He replied.

"So who are you?" she pressed.

The man took a deep breath "It's not easy to explain." he confessed.

"I did create the universe so the best description of me from your point of view, is 'The Creator'. A mite egotistical I must admit but it's an accurate statement."

"So what are you?" She pressed.

The man put his fingertips together and thought for a moment. "This is going to sound patronising, but there's no way that I can explain that to you from your frame of reference."

"How can I believe that you are the creator then?" she continued. "If you were, you'd know everything about the universe and everything that's in it...actually you'd know everything about me."

"Correct," he replied and before she had a chance to speak he pressed on. "I do know everything about you. You love cats but don't like ginger ones but you don't know why, you adore the smell of newly mown grass, the best sex you ever had was with a mining engineer on Phobos, you have a freckle behind your left ear and when you first saw the earth from orbit it was less impressive than you expected. You prefer to sleep on your left side and you still feel guilty about stamping on a spider that you found in your cupboard when your family moved to New York. You feel that your nose is the least attractive thing about your body and you had the hots for your father's best friend when you were a teenager...how am I doing? Do you want more?"

The astronaut reacted as if she had been struck physically "That's enough," she said quietly.

The old man chuckled. "Sorry about that but I had to give you stuff that would bring you up to speed quickly...and don't worry...I most certainly don't judge you, in fact I can't judge you as that defeats the exercise and would also be self destructive. You're part of me you see. I looked inside myself and you were what I found...you and a whole universe. I don't judge you...I experience you...in fact I experience everything....that's what this is all about."

The woman just stared. She had rarely ever been speechless, but she had so many questions and didn't know which to ask first. Sensing this the old man continued. "Yes, I know, it's a lot to take on board isn't it? Only a few have ever made it this far and they've had the same problems.

"Which few?" She said; glad to have something apparently rational to talk about.

"Oh you weren't the only species to have figured out faster than light travel; actually you're the fourth, shall we say, 'being,' to make the trip."

"So why." she said. "Why the universe? What do you mean, 'you experience me?'"

The old man leaned back on his chair. "You asked me early on what I was and I told you you wouldn't understand the answer. The truth is I don't fully know myself. I know that I am and that I exist but that's all I really know. I know I am powerful and I feel….God do I *feel*….err sorry… probably the wrong phrase to use….but I exist without a universe…I exist in timeless harmony. I need to experience what I am…to know what I am…I know I am what you call 'good' but if I don't experience it how can I fully understand that about myself? I need to know, you see…I need to know all of it…so I created the universe from my very being. It's all part of me and I'm part of it. I created an environment with linear time and countless races and 'possibilities,' which I could experience through those entities that inhabit it."

She thought for a moment and asked the obvious question. "Why did you have to create the pain and suffering…death, disease, conflict, cruelty…the universe can be a really shitty place. Why didn't you create somewhere… well…nice?"

The old man pursed his lips and sucked regretfully thorough his teeth. "I know," he said gently. "It can be hard, even unbearable, but I had to… don't you see? This is what it's all about. To know myself as good I had to create what you call 'bad' to experience the opposite of what I am to know what I am."

She came back quicker than he expected. "Isn't that just bloody selfish? We have to suffer so that you can go on your little voyage of self-discovery? Countless trillions suffer just so you can 'find yourself'?"

"Hmmmmm," the old man said. "I see that I'm going to have to try a little harder to convince you that my quest is beneficial to all. You see, I've told you that you're part of me, therefore you don't die nor does anyone; you just come back to me. But you're asking yourself, what does coming 'back to me' really mean? I think it's time for some of the real stuff. Some things are only understood by experience...they cannot be explained. He made to move his hand when she snapped, "Wait a minute, whatever you're going to do or show me, I need to know something first. If you're not God, despite the fact that you seem to know everything and evidently created everything, then that means that you're telling me that there is no God."

He laughed again his eyes twinkling as he enjoyed his reverie "Oh no, Commodore, there most certainly is a God...I created all this to *know* God." And with that their environment exploded. A mass of incredible white brightness engulfed them both. In that instant the astronaut had no body; she was existence only. She felt the old man, she felt herself....she felt the universe...she felt *everything*. For an instant of time she knew and experienced that she was 'all that is,' the power of the experience beyond her ability to describe it. Her psyche opened, really opened, allowing her to understand for the first time the power of everything. She saw the unique dynamics of emotion and understood why they were real and the physical world was not. She called out as if experiencing a thousand orgasms simultaneously. She *felt*...for the first time she truly *felt*. "Oh my God," she gasped, "I had no idea...I had no idea...this is what I am...I remember....I remember....oh my God, oh my God, oh my God!" And it that instant it was gone. She was a sat on her chair again opposite the man, sobbing uncontrollably. As her body racked with tears she blurted out "You love me...you know everything about me but you love me anyway...I remember." The man pulled her out of the chair and embraced her gently as she continued sobbing into his shoulder.

She stayed there for what seemed like a very long time. Eventually he released his hold on her and fixed her with a look that made her feel transparent. A feeling that she found totally pleasurable. She had no secrets...he *knew* her. He whispered in her ear, "How could I not love you? We are one and the same. You are part of me as I am part of you. I am also part of something bigger, which means you are part of it too which means it is part of you as well. In existence there is infinite bigness and infinite smallness; it goes all the way up and all the way down... for infinity. We're all the same thing. To know what we are we must experience ourselves. This is what we are doing...this is what we're all doing...we all seek to know ourselves."

Exhausted, she flopped back onto the chair "There's so much I want to ask...so much I need to know," she said quietly.

The old man smiled. "When you have taught a child to add two and two the next lesson is not advanced equations...remembering is best done stage by stage...a gradual process."

She let a silence hang in the air for a moment. "So what happens now?"

The doctors had assured her she wouldn't dream, but they were so wrong. These were the first thoughts that occurred to the astronaut as she began her slow wake from hibernation.

- The End -

A GLIMPSE

Things hadn't been the same since the operation. Not that they'd been bad, far from it, but, certainly, they were different.

The good news was that the tumour had been removed successfully. It had apparently been touch and go on the operating table, but she'd pulled through. He had suffered the agonies of the damned as he worried about her. By the time she had the operation she hardly noticed. She was actually suffering the agonies of the damned physically. The headaches nearly driving her insane with their intensity. 'Knives cleaving at her brain' was the way she'd described it. It had made him sick just to think about it.

Mercifully, that was now all behind her and them. He had his wife back. She was well, she was vibrant and she was delighted to be alive. And she was different. Not in a bad way, but certainly it made things difficult for him. At first he hadn't cared so pleased was he that she was healthy. It had taken a while to notice but things had definitely changed.

Her withering sarcasm that he found so attractive had gone. She also didn't seem to find his own creatively scathing criticisms of others amusing as she once had. She also laughed a lot more now. Not the occasional sly sniggers she affected prior to the operation, but big, wholesome belly laughs. Long gone also were her amusing tirades about her workmate's shortcomings. He sincerely missed those. She used to have such an acerbic wit about her. She saw the humour in cruel teasing. It was one of the things that had attracted him to her. She had shared his bleak cynicism of the world and others. He wasn't a bad or insensitive man, but he was a realist and so she used to be.

In the bedroom things had changed too. Their love making, whilst physically satisfying was now, so, well, what was the word? Wholesome. Yes, that was it, wholesome. Not a bad thing he supposed. They'd always been creative, and still were but now she seemed to relish every new permutation as a natural progression and not a daring adventure, which somehow took the frission of excitement away.

And then there were the silences. Now she would often be quiet when in the past she'd chattered continually. Car journeys were a case in point. They'd rarely played music as their banter would provide all the entertainment they required. Now, all too often, he'd turn the radio on to cover up the lack of conversation.

Of course they'd discussed it. Nothing was actually wrong per se but she agreed she felt different. The trouble was that he didn't. And, she confessed, she felt that the change was accelerating. Not only that, she was enjoying the changes. She said she felt alive as if never before. She said she could see things differently. She said she needed to see where these changes were taking her. This worried him. The woman he loved was becoming a different person. He didn't want to think of where this would lead. Surely he should love her no matter what? He wrestled with this dilemma. His wife had lost her cynicism. She'd developed a sense of humour that seemed to him to border on the childish. Her delightful scowls and dark biting tongue were a thing of the past. He missed them, and missed them badly.

She was genuinely distressed at the effect she was having on her husband. She seemed delighted at the changes within her and yet her love for her partner demanded she addressed his concerns. She was as curious as he to identify the cause of these changes.

Various professionals had relieved them of large sums of money whilst providing no answers. Undeterred, he continued to seek answers. She uncomplainingly went along with his research while developing a lust for life that he found almost unbearable in its enthusiasm. The nadir came at the hypnotist's office.

She'd approached the session with such a boundless rapture he'd almost considered cancelling it. Prior to the operation, at even the suggestion of such an encounter, she would have heaped a withering diatribe on him for even suggesting it. God, he missed that. He loved that about her.

In a darkened room, the bearded Freudian swung his watch as his wife succumbed to the calming, suggestive voice.

"I want you to go back," he whispered, "back to the moment of change."

There was silence for a full minute. Suddenly his wife's face lit up. "The operation," she almost shouted.

"Tell us about it," the hypnotist urged.

Though her eyes were closed he could see anticipation on his wife's face.

"The anaesthetist asked me to count back from ten to one. I knew I'd never reach one but I thought it would be fun to try. I reached six and then suddenly I was just floating. Floating in space. I felt like Superman. I could fly. It was just wonderful." She lapsed into silence with a calm smile on her face.

"Please continue," the therapist prompted.

She took a very deep breath. "I travelled, faster and faster, past stars and galaxies. I travelled so fast they all became a blur. I just knew that I had to keep going. I wasn't afraid; I was enthralled. I don't know how I knew I had to keep going but something inside told me that I had somewhere to go. I knew that something was waiting for me at my destination. Something important." She paused for a moment as if steeling herself, then pressed on.

"I suddenly came to a stop. Incredibly, there was a wall in front of me. I knew immediately what it was. I just had to get over it, to see what was inside. It was so annoying. No matter which direction I flew the wall was there. It seemed to stretch forever upwards and downwards." She paused again.

"Why did you have to get over the wall?" The husband immediately felt ashamed at his outburst.

"To see what was on the other side. You see, I knew," she said.

Ignoring the hypnotist's dark stare, he pressed on, "What did you know? What was on the other side?"

His wife laughed. "Why, Heaven of course, you silly thing. It was so frustrating. No matter how far I flew in any direction there was no door, no way in. Then I noticed out of the corner of my eye, just below me, a bright point of light. I was sure that it wasn't there before. I swooped down to it for a closer look. It was a small hole, no bigger than my little finger. A hole in Heaven." Her breathing accelerated. "I realised at once I could look in. I pressed my eye over the hole and…I saw Heaven…I saw inside Heaven…I saw…" Her voice seemed to peter out as she relaxed back into her chair, her face serenely calm.

Agitated, her husband addressed her urgently, "What did you see? What did you see?"

She opened her eyes and fixed him with a look of such wonder he would never ever find the words to describe it.

"Everything," she said.

- The End -

ABRACADABRA

He certainly hadn't climbed to the top of the greasy pole of success via a route that could ever be described as traditional. Not that he cared. It was the cash that counted and now he had more than he could count. He used to take it from people without them knowing. Now he took it from them with his victim's full knowledge he was conning them. The switch amused him. Though cynical beyond belief he appreciated irony. At least that was real.

With an extravagant flourish he covered the scantily clad, tightly bound girl with a satin cloth. The drums rolled, the lights dimmed, then, a moment later, a bright explosion of smoke shook the stage and the girl vanished. Incredibly, seconds later, the spotlight swooped to the back of the huge auditorium revealing the girl, miraculously unbound, running back down through the aisles of people, back to the stage to thunderous applause. 'Jesus,' he thought, 'haven't these people ever heard of twins?' Their gullibility made him despise their weakness. There was the irony again. It was their weakness that had made him rich.

As he began to surreptitiously attach himself to the ultra fine cables would facilitate his 'flying' finale, he was vaguely aware that he was bored. God, was he bored. He desperately missed the excitement of the early days, when he'd begun on the journey of learning his craft. Unlike most magicians he hadn't wasted his childhood endlessly practicing pathetic tricks or spending his allowance on cheap parlour illusions. This wasn't what had interested him. He realised early in life that misdirection and manipulative skill could be used to his advantage. Not for him the junior magician's circle or the appreciation of his classmates at a spectacular vanish. He embraced sleight of hand and deception. By the age of eleven he was already grifting in the school playground, effortlessly relieving people of lunch money. By thirteen he was unbeatable at poker. Whether it be a marked deck, card counting, crooked dealing or sometimes just his rigorously trained memory, he was able to totally control every encounter. In his hands, playing cards did his bidding. Endless practice paid off. Chance simply didn't come into it. Only a fool would believe in luck.

While he was fleecing his classmates, safe in the knowledge that he could never lose, he also acquired the skills of watching for the bluff. The 'shows' and 'tells' that his friends exhibited in their amateurish attempts to deceive. It gave him valuable knowledge and experience of people and how they could be manipulated. At sixteen he could read people as easily as the daily paper.

His stack of cash began to turn from modest into something more substantial as he saw the rewards of his practice. He moved from cards to 'dips', 'lifts' and 'brushes'. His ability to deprive friends and classmates of their cash by nudging against them or by a deft piece of misdirection became a daily occurrence. His prey would have enjoyed his skill, if he'd ever told them what he'd done. He never did. He then made the jump to strangers on the street and the money really began to roil in,

His hands, eyes and quick brain became his most valuable assets. He investigated thoroughly the experiences he had whilst observing the gullible and the victims of his skills. He then delved into the money pit that was clairvoyance, prediction and mentalism. There, with his well-honed observational skills and phenomenal memory, he made a name for himself amongst those who desperately wanted to believe in his gift. It was an easy sell. After all, he believed in them. They were making him rich.

The wealthier he became the more curious he was at the seemingly endless ways that people could be deceived. He mastered the intricate technicalities of 'vanishes', 'palming' and the 'skim'. How to make a roomful of people see what he wanted them to see. How to influence their thinking simply by the power of his own mind and personality. He moved effortlessly to hypnotism. He was able to mesmerise the most vulnerable subjects in seconds. His ability to identify those subjects was refined to a fine art as his quest continued.

By eighteen he was not merely an enviably talented magician, he was an increasingly affluent and professional con man. He saw no difference between the two. As his success continued, his arrogance grew until the day he made a spectacularly disastrous share trade. Wiped out overnight, he was forced to complement his grifting by performing table magic at novelty restaurants. It was a crushing blow. He took his revenge on his stockbroker by lifting his wallet six times in as many weeks, together with his car and house keys on two additional occasions. The havoc he caused in the man's life gave him at least some recompense.

As he performed a particularly innovative vanish at a table one night (the tips were better if he made an effort) his smooth technique and darkly cynical patter came to the notice of one of the diners at another table. As he was about to move on, the man blocked his path and pressed a business card into his hand. "Hey, Kid," he smiled. "Call me." He turned to return to his seat. As the conjurer studied his card the diner looked back at him and winked, "*Abracadabra* huh?" Momentarily non-plussed the magician looked up, "Yeah, sure, *Abracadabra.*"

As he sat in the agent's office two days later his mood was in high spirits. Five confiscated billfolds tended to have that effect. It had been a good morning and it was still only eleven o'clock. "OK," the agent demanded, "Show me what ya got." Twenty minutes later the man was astounded by the competence of the performance he'd witnessed. It was one of the best he'd ever seen. The brief show was combination of flawless close up magic, mentalism and a vicious patter seemingly engineered to humiliate him. A real crowd pleaser; people loved to see others embarrassed. His level of skill was extraordinary. Yep, the kid had it. He signed him on the spot. As the ink was drying on the contract he fixed the young man with a gimlet eye. "Study your craft. Really study it. We'll make a killing." Together with the share tip it was the only advice he ever took. He was glad he did.

He rose rapidly through the ranks. His unique act stunning and appalling audiences in equal measure. In the mentalsim part of his show, his exposure of his suspects knew no bounds. He revealed details that should not just have been shut away, but buried in coffins six feet deep in the ground then covered in concrete. His hypnosis show was so extreme that minors were banned from attending. His conjuring amazed people with its audacity and innovation. In these moments the audience forgot his cruelty and gawped in fascination. Once he started to perform they were caught like rabbits in his headlights. Cannon fodder.

Naturally, lawsuits followed, the publicity droving his booking fees ever skywards. There was even a high profile suicide. The money cascaded in. Business was good. He was loathed and adored in equal measure. He delved into his craft ever deeper in the knowledge that the greater his skill the greater the rewards. His only pleasure came from his ever more brutal manipulation of his audiences; simultaneously striking them speechless with wonder at his illusions whilst ritually verbally abusing those he selected from the adoring crowds.

'Who the fuck are 'The League?' was the first thought that had come to mind when he picked up the envelope in his post box. The paper was of a quality that told him this wasn't junk mail. Additionally, his name and address had been written in a flourishing hand. On the top left hand corner of the lush manila stationary, 'The League' was monogrammed in an impressive embossed typeface. Curious, he opened it and read.

'You are summoned to appear before the League to account for your behaviour. Call this number to make an appointment. Do not delay.'

It was unsigned. Save for a telephone number beneath the message, the missive contained no further information. He read the message a second time, briefly bemused. His attention wavered and then, annoyed at the intrusion, he tore it up. An identical letter arrived the following day. And the next. And the next.

On the fifth day, as he was tearing up yet another entreaty, his doorbell sounded.

The man who stood in his doorway was immaculately dressed. An exquisitely cut suit complimented by a perfect yet incongruous Lily in the buttonhole of his lapel. Apparently in his late sixties replete with a shining bald scalp, the man was staring at him with what appeared to be curiosity. "Yes?" the magician snapped irritably. The man looked down at the Lily and appeared to study it carefully. "I always wear one of these. It's an ancient symbol of innocence and purity."

"And that's of relevance to me how?" The conjurer exhibited his well-known short fuse.

"The craft that we practice needs be to gentle, lest we are tempted take advantage of the innocent, those souls who give themselves over to our skills in their belief of our power. The purity the Lily represents symbolises this wondrous web of magic we weave and its true origins. Thus I wear this flower to constantly remind me of these two truths."

The magician scoffed, "Who the fuck uses words like 'lest' and 'thus'? Jesus, man. Just fuck off why don't you?" He made to shut the door. At that moment a picture fell off the wall behind him with a loud crash, startling him. In the moment he hesitated, the man entered. Momentarily confused, he was about to speak when the stranger beat him to it. "Actually, I thought I'd come in."

The two men stood facing each other, the stranger was looking at him intently. He had the most compelling eyes. As the magician looked into them the room seemed to shudder slightly. In a second he recognised the signs and then he was back and actually laughed. "Hey, that was pretty good," he said. "I'm a stone cold hostile subject and you got me to stage one." As he spoke the man held up his hand. It held the magician's wallet. "Good lift," the conjurer admitted. "Now give it back and get out." The stranger threw the wallet into the air, where it burst into flames before it hit the ground. As it touched the carpet, it crumbled into ash.

The conjurer was impressed in spite of himself. A most professional dip, followed by a full sight switch in bright light and instant remote combustion, all close up. He hadn't caught the dip and certainly not the switch. "Because you weren't looking for them," said the stranger, reading his thoughts. "I caught you unawares. Now you're aware. Watch this."

He reached inside his suit pocket and produced a handkerchief. He methodically and precisely began to unfold it. The conjurer was instantly bored, but something inside him told him to keep looking. The man continued to unfold the handkerchief. He continued to unfold it until the magician realised that this was no normal piece of cloth. Thirty seconds later the stranger held up sash of material that was taller and wider than he was. He held it up in front of him at each of the top corners, with only his hands now visible to the magician. A moment later he saw the man's hands release the cloth and it fell to the floor, the stranger behind it now gone. The conjurer was stunned. He was even more stunned to hear a quiet cough behind him. He spun round to see his uninvited guest sitting on a sofa.

It took him five seconds. What he'd seen was impossible. "You got me to stage two, you clever bastard. Bring me out of it now," he demanded. The stranger smiled. "You're not under. Surely you don't believe that you could be mesmerised that quickly?" The truth was, he didn't. He wasn't susceptible. He knew the tricks of the trade. The stranger spoke again, interrupting his thoughts "I'm here representing the League," he said.

The man had his attention. That he had to admit. "You have five minutes," he snapped.

"Very well," his guest nodded. "You've rather rudely been ignoring our invitations. Actually, you've been rather rude generally. We've decided that it's got to stop."

He continued, "the League has been in existence, in some form or another, since the very beginnings of magic. It was formed initially as a forum where those who practiced could come together in the company of like-minded individuals to exchange ideas. It's always been a secret of course. Secrets are the source of our power. That much I know you understand. The forum evolved over time as a keeper of these great secrets, and to keep the practitioners and the very greatest exponents of our art close to the true spirit of the power we possess. To entertain and to do good for those who would hold us in awe. To encourage responsibility in those blessed in the craft."

The magician laughed, "Yeah right. Then why haven't I heard about you then?"

The stranger leaned forward. "Because, my young friend, you are not a great conjurer. You have not even started. When measured against the likes of Keller, Thurston, Houdini or Blackstone you are merely a flim flam man. A gaudy and unsophisticated charlatan too caught up in his own naked greed to even begin to understand the elegance of your chosen profession. And I'm only mentioning names that you'll know. The vast majority of the League are not even in the public eye. This has always been our way. We are the keepers, the guardians of the gift."

The magician reacted in fury. "A flim flam man? I'm the biggest fucking name in the business! Don't come round here lecturing me about a sad bunch of amateurs jerking off in private pretending all this is real. We do tricks. We con people because they're too weak minded to work out how we do it. That's it, pure and simple."

Unmoved, the stranger answered him. "Is it? What is real magic? If you perform a spectacular vanish that no one can fathom, then it's magic to the observer."

"Yeah," interrupted the magician, "It's magic to them not to us. That's the real gig. We know it's not real."

"Magic is all around us," his guest offered carefully. "It's constantly present. Sometimes recognised and sometimes not. You and I and a few select others have the ability to tap into it. We have a responsibility."

"No we don't," argued the conjurer. "We're just deceivers. We have no responsibility. Their pathetic weakness provides us with a living. That's it. End of story."

"We don't feel the same way," the stranger murmured. "We'd rather like you to fall in line and stop being such a bore. You do show so much promise."

"Promise?" barked the magician. "I could buy you out of small change"

"I seriously doubt it," the stranger responded, "Speaking of small change, do you have any? I want to show you something I think you'll rather like." Grudgingly, the conjurer pulled four coins from his pocket and placed them on a coffee table in front of the stranger, who picked them up and stared at them thoughtfully. "Did you know that the word 'magic' derives from the ancient Greek word 'magi' which was used to describe…"

The magician butted in, "Yeah, I know, the magi were a bunch of Babylonians who were thought to have the power to control demons and the like. It was a religious gig. I know my stuff for Christ's sakes."

"I suspect not as well as you think," the stranger spoke quietly. "These Babylonians followed a great teacher called Zoroaster, a very wise man who based his teachings on three principles. Maybe you recall them? Good reflection, good word, and good deeds. In the League we do our best to uphold these principles. And, whilst we are tolerant men and women by nature, sometimes these principles need defending more robustly than we would normally feel comfortable with. That's why I'm here. You are enormously talented. If you, well, adapted, it would be most beneficial, especially for you. All that we ask is that you affect a measure of consideration and gentleness in your performance and attitude. We have no problem with you profiting from your endeavours, but to quote the good Lord. "To whom much is given, much is expected."

The magician didn't even hesitate. "Don't even think of bringing fucking religion into this. 'To whom much is given?' Nobody ever gave me anything pal. All I have is the result of hard work. Why are you giving me all this cosmic bullshit? We just do tricks. I'm on the gravy train. I've got a first class one way ticket."

The stranger started passing the coins between his hands. "Are you saying there's no way that I can influence you to stop bringing our craft into disrepute? Are you really so convinced that we're all just con artists? Are you committed to the principle that our skilful and elegant presentations are merely smoke and mirrors? I'd heard you had no redeeming features but I refused to believe it. It's in my nature to seek out the best in people. That's why The League charged me to make this visit. I thought I could make a difference. Is your current course unstoppable? Have I failed?"

The magician was now irritated. The man's words bounced off him like drops of rain. "Are you going to do a trick with those coins or not?"

With a shrug of resignation, his guest laid the four coins out on the table in front of him. He muttered an incantation under his breath, and as the magician watched, the four coins rose into the air and hovered in front of him. It was good, he had to admit. "Want to check for wires?" enquired the stranger. Intrigued, he approached the floating coins and traced his hands around them. No wires. He was impressed. No, he was more than impressed. He reached out to pluck one of the apparently floating coins from the air. As he touched the first one, it vanished. Just like that. One minute it was there and the next it wasn't. He instinctively reached for the next coin. At that moment the remaining three also vanished. The magician blinked in amazement and then laughed.

"That was fucking good, Abracadabra man! Oh, and by the way, that comes from an Aramaic phrase *avra kehdabra*. It means, "I will create as I speak.""

"Actually, my young unrepentant friend, it's a far older incantation, but I do agree it's an appropriate phrase to use after the execution of this trick. Let me demonstrate." He looked up and thrust a bony finger in the magician's direction. "Abracadabra!" he shouted.

The magician burst into flames. In a moment, like his wallet before him, he was a pile of ash on the carpet.

The stranger stood up. "As I said, it's a far more ancient spell. It's actually from the Babylonian *abbada ke dabra*. It means, 'Perish like the word.'"

- The End -

THE PROGRAM

She'd never flunked out of a program before and she certainly wasn't going to flunk out of this one. It just wasn't her way. She'd push till it broke. And it always did such was the force of her perseverance.

It was this single-minded attitude that had enabled her to go so very far. Further even than her greatest mentors had ever predicted or could have even imagined. Her parents, her professors, her instructors and guides would be shocked to know how far she'd gone. An irony of course. Even if they had have known they could never even begin to actually comprehend where she now found herself.

Her journey had been a long one though she now preferred the term 'quest'. Despite being blessed/cursed with a deep beauty, she'd never bought into the human myth, preferring instead intellectual challenges and an undisguised wonder about the nature of existence itself. As far back as she could remember she'd wanted and needed to experience the unusual and unique and, occasionally, the extreme. The mundane constraints of terrestrial existence held no attraction for her. Study was her purview. To understand, to learn, to question relentlessly as opposed to accepting the norm. Not for her a husband, children and the prison that they represented. Not that she eschewed love and ecstasy. She embraced them, savoured them and relished the release and altered states they could engender. Sadly her unabashed hedonism intimidated most of those she allowed close. The men and women whom she shared it with inevitably fell into the time-honoured trap of adoration or loathing, through lack of understanding or the need to possess. It didn't help that she pushed those close to her as much as she pushed herself. She needed to know, to comprehend and would accept no boundaries, even in relationships and especially in intimacy. Under this barrage people continually disappointed her, but she felt able to live with it. There were more important things demanding her attention.

From the time she was able to walk she knew she needed to fly. It was a first stage, she reasoned. A first stage in leaving the mundane constraints and trivia of human existence. She took her first flying lesson on her sixteenth birthday.

Existence, she had come to understand, was about moments. Some moments were more significant than others. At least that was what she once thought. She now knew that this was simply an observational function. Moments, and their significance, merely reflected the state of mind of the person experiencing them. This profound understanding was not yet part of her rationale when she went solo for the first time.

She'd lined up the flimsy Cessna into the wind on the grass airfield. With a mounting excitement she'd released the toe brakes, opened the throttle and commenced her bouncy take off run in the woefully underpowered aeroplane. Not that that mattered. The moment her wheels left the ground her rapture threatened to overcome her. She was free. For the next thirty minutes she skipped though the clouds in a state of near Zen like tranquillity. The freedom sucked her in with its enchanting soothing embrace. She was never the same again.

From that moment on she plunged into the books with a rapaciousness that even had her teachers concerned about the almost fanatical level of her dedication. They didn't understand. In those thirty minutes of solo flight she'd finally caught a glimpse of true liberation, of something different, something not related to the trivialities of an Earth bound existence. This was what she had been seeking. Wonder, awe and release. Release to express that which she was. Or at least, that which she thought she was.

Her single mindedness knew no boundaries. As time went by she grew increasingly irritated by humanity and the lack of quality candidates to share her and her dreams. She was equally slack jawed with what she perceived as the lack of substance of the dreams of those she met. She now realised that she had been judgmental, and that she'd not understood enough to comprehend the fine line between pity and compassion. At the time she had brushed off such thoughts as she focused relentlessly on her goals. Despite the enormous barriers put in her way, she succeeded in achieving her objectives.

She recalled the time that when she'd felt that only specific moments were important. After her Cessna flight, the next such occasion was during a perfect afternoon in the middle of the Sea of Japan. Her gloved hands feathered the throttles of her twitchy F14 Tomcat fighter as she turned into the downward leg of her final approach to the floating city that was the *USS Nimitz*. A floating city it may have been but from her position it looked like a matchbox. Fear rose up inside her and gripped her. It thrilled her with its impact. Her Ivy League education hadn't prepared her for this. Her first carrier landing. She fought the pitching monster, managing its immense power as the warm air rising from the ocean buffeted her and her charge. When she'd eventually hit the cold hard steel of the carrier deck, perfectly hooking the arrestor wire and decelerating from 140 miles per hour to zero in 150 yards, it was all she could do not to scream out loud in ecstasy. Strapping a fast jet to her back had been the ultimate rush. So far. Within three years it had palled. She needed more.

Emotionally she needed more too. Increasingly irritated by the limitations and constraints of her physical and professional relationships, she plunged with abandon into spirituality. She absorbed new age and traditionalist teachings with an almost manic possession. Jaded by the restrictions of military flying, she left the Navy and embraced the hallowed halls of Caltech. There she immersed herself in the mysteries of astrophysics and cosmology and the unique elegance they offered. She walked with intellectual giants and opened herself up to their awesome knowledge. She delved into the insights of Fermi, Einstein, Feynman and Hawking and let their lustre brush off on her.

Four years later, with yet another master's degree to her name, she realised that her own education had only just begun. Even as she received her degree certificate, she knew it was, as indeed were all things, simply a collection of protons and neutrons spinning around, their electro magnetic fields giving the illusion of reality. As a result of her studies she now also understood that the entire universe was equally empty and bereft of what most would refer to as substance…but not meaning.

Now she knew more, she knew that she knew even less than she had ever expected. The meaningless of time, the fact that space was composed of virtually nothing and that within that empty vortex, humanity apparently existed. What was humanity? What was she? Why was anything anything? To even begin to understand the universe and her place in it, she knew she needed to experience more of it. She immersed herself with new vigour in the study of her spirituality, and embarked on yet another new demanding program.

As the shuttle reached apogee, the first rays of the ever-rising sun came over the curvature of the Earth. The first time she ever saw it she thought her heart would stop such was the beauty of the moment. Ignoring the scene she gently nudged the liquid fuel manoeuvring thrusters, turning the vehicle into the correct vector for re entry. Her eyes executed a practiced sweep over the various readouts, noting with satisfaction that the gimbal rates were congruent with her own calculations. Down range, Mission Control advised her that she was go for descent. With one last wistful look at the heavens above her, the shuttle commander carefully edged her charge into the controlled fall that would take her and her crew back to earth.

As she was violently shaken by the enormous friction of the descent into the atmosphere, she felt almost detached. It was her third time and second as commander. She knew she'd gone as far as she could. She'd seen and experienced the very limit of human endeavour and reached as far out into the cosmos as she was ever going to. *It wasn't enough!*

There was one last occasion before she stopped looking at specific moments as being important and realised that they were all important. It was after five years of study in a bitterly cold monastery on the outskirts of Osaka in Southern Japan. It was also at the end of one of the most challenging programs she'd ever set herself.

At the end of a particularly exhausting day, she'd stumbled into her Roshi's enclave, her legs numb from eight hours of straight Zazen meditation. Eight hours of continual mental interrogation into the conundrum given to students by their instructors. A mental conundrum so obscure it was designed so that the very act of interrogating it would enable the mind to go beyond itself and allow true enlightenment to occur. True paradoxes to be meditated upon. These apparently bizarre puzzles were called *Koans*. Hers was a classic: *What was your face before your parents were born?*

Her head and body aching from the concentration, she sat stiffly in front of her instructor for her daily interview session. Despite her physical exhaustion, her mind was unusually alert and focused. "What is Zen?" he barked at her. Something about his tone seemed to rip into her head. For reasons that she didn't understand at the time, she just smiled at him. "Good," her master murmured.

The Roshi indicated his flowing robe. "Is this material Zen?" he asked, more gently this time.

"It cannot be," she answered with confidence.

"And why is that?" her interrogator demanded.

With a sudden total clarity she answered. As she spoke she heard her words as if someone else were saying them. "It cannot be Zen, therefore it must be. Zen is that which it is not, therefore it must be that which it is." Alert now, her Roshi saw that the moment was almost upon her. "Are you Zen?" he asked, almost so quietly she had difficulty making out his words.

Like a dying star she literally felt her mind collapsing in on itself. She heard her voice, distant and disembodied.

"Zen is an expression of that which is beyond expression. Zen does not exist, so therefore it must exist. I am that which I am, therefore I am not that which I am not and I am not that which I am."

Deliberately pushing, the Roshi shouted at her. "You're talking in riddles. Have you learned nothing? Are you Zen or not?" He saw the look on her face change and he knew she was teetering on the brink.

She exhaled deeply. A single tear ran down her cheek. "There is no Zen. There is nothing at all."

The collapsing star of her mind reached a point of zero volume and infinite density, and like a star, in that moment it went supernova.

In that moment she *was*. Gone in that instant were the façades and constraints that mankind allowed its physically to suggest were reality. Her very being reached the ends of existence itself. It did so because she saw that she *was* existence itself. She started laughing, laughing at her life. She saw the sublime humour in the deep dichotomies of space-time and relativity. She laughed at her attempts to master the intracies of these paradoxes. She laughed at the cosmic joke, a joke that she'd made up herself and then allowed herself to forget the punch line in order to enjoy the experience of rediscovering it.

In that moment of timelessness she saw her life with a deep love. She recalled a line from Paramahansa Yogananda that expressed the sensation to perfection. *An oceanic joy broke upon calm endless shores of my soul.* She laughed again as she realised she was Paramahansa and that Paramahansa did not exist, as she'd made him up, as indeed he'd made her up. Therefore, she couldn't exist either. A delicious dichotomy, yet now to her perfectly understandable. An unrestrained love pounded through her. Indeed she comprehended that it *was* her. It was what she was. It was all there was. In that instant she needed to express this, so exquisite was the sensation. She reached out in her bliss and saw she could do this in any way she wished. She relished the fact that she now remembered that the rediscovery of the truth was part of the joy of the truth itself. It always had been. It was what she had been doing forever.

It was time to set herself a new program. She anticipated the delicious adventure.

This time she'd make it *really* difficult to remember.

- The End -

CONSEQUENCES

That he loved her was the one true certainty in his existence. Indeed, he knew his love for her was so strong it actually defined that which he was. When apart, his being ached for her, so unbearable was the experience. He could almost not remember a time when he had not known her and now even the thought of that far off time gave him hurt. The pain of his non-completeness before he had encountered her still lingered. Now, so perfect was their union, he found it difficult to define where he ended and she began. Her very beingness engulfed him totally. The stark contrast of her sublime femininity entwined perfectly with his representation of masculinity. He regarded her as way beyond being his partner...she was fifty percent of one entity...a delicious symbiosis where the equation equalled bliss.

He considered the statement, *a delicious symbiosis where the equation equalled bliss.* It was an insight that gave him satisfaction. It was as a result of equations that they had come together, a shared interest that lesser minds referred to as mathematics and physics. The truth was, as they had grown and worked together, they had long passed the mere intellectual interrogation of quantum and celestial mechanics and had moved, with a perfect union of thought, into realms of comprehending and quantifying the very dynamics of existence itself.

Her passion for him was all consuming. Her first love had been questioning that which was at the wild frontier where science collides with metaphysics. His intellect had invaded her psyche with a jarring shock that had left her dizzy with its effect. Numbed by this welcome and unique intrusion, she had joined with him and experienced a depth of feeling she knew immediately she could never lack again. When he was with her she was complete, pure and simple. They had journeyed beyond passion and love…they now simply *were*. Their relationship existed in the realm where words were inadequate.

And now, when they worked and thought together, they vibrated in perfect unison. They no longer considered equations…they *felt* them. In harmony they now saw the intricate lattices that made up the subtle harmonics of being. They had actually begun to *feel* the beautiful simplicity of the complexity that held the very fabric of existence together. They had begun to unlock the very secrets of what *was*. Their progress in this bold intellectual adventure served only to bring them even closer together, a closeness that was as almost unbearable as it was delicious.

It was as they came closer to grasping and quantifying the greatest mysteries of 'all that is' that the unbearableness grew. It grew not as dissatisfaction, but as a realisation they had experienced their love in every way possible. So strong was their love that they sought further infinite ways of expressing it.

Unsurprisingly, they discovered the answers to their questions simultaneously. In a unique moment of revelation, they grasped the solution to their investigations of existence and their unrequited desire to find a further unique tableau in which to experience the infinite diversity of their love. They came together as one and called out a request.

And…a moment later…there *was* light.

- The End -

THE BUTTON

Warrior one, warrior two, reverse warrior, down into plank, upward dog, downwards facing dog. The man ran through the regime in his mind as he put himself through the yoga session in his cramped cabin. At least he had a cabin and he was grateful for that. The majority of his one hundred and fifty crew did not. Despite the size of the fleet's newest nuclear submarine, some things remained forever the bane of the professional submariner, a lack of space being one of them.

He caught sight of himself in the mirror. A bead of sweat hung comically from the end of his nose as he concentrated on a particularly challenging pose. He didn't look stressed. He was trying not to be stressed. A lot of people were counting on him not to be stressed. He shut out the thoughts and delved further into his practice.

As the captain continued his session, the *USS Louisiana* slipped silently though the deep waters of the South China Sea. Its sleek shape made short work of the strong undercurrents and eddies, as the powerful reactor churned out vast kilojoules of energy to the single massive propeller at its rear.

She was the newest (and maybe the last) of the great leviathans of the deep. One point five billion dollars of high tech hardware squeezed into a mere five hundred and fifty foot length. Nineteen thousand tons of cold steel, bristling with revolutionary electronics and a weapons package that was almost too terrible to contemplate, she was the ultimate deterrent. Virtually undetectable, her job was to prowl the seas in the knowledge that her very existence ensured those with designs against U.S. interests would think twice. She was, in navel parlance, a *Boomer*, laden with Trident missiles tipped with nuclear warheads, the powers of which were unthinkable. She was the ultimate peacekeeper.

Not everyone was impressed. Certain people in Mainland China thought she was a bluff. The Chinese were a nation of gamblers. Unlike the more pragmatic Russians during the cold war, the Chinese tended to call bluffs. After all, they reasoned, would the United States really go to war over Taiwan?

Some hawks in the U.S. military believed the Chinese were arrogant enough to call the bluff. Some could not believe that they would be stupid enough to do so. The Chinese reasoned the time had never been better to re take the island. With the U.S. public weary with the debacle that was Iraq and U.S. forces stretched ever more thinly through the Middle East and Afghanistan, their gambler's ethic suggested that maybe their moment had arrived. In Washington, supposedly wise minds argued both ways.

None of the politics entered the captain's mind as he arrived at the con for the start of his watch. He had to concentrate totally on the operations of the ship and it's state of readiness for whatever was to come. Some five hundred feet above him and many miles to the south, the aircraft carrier *USS Ronald Regan* pounded through the waves leading the mammoth carrier group to its prearranged station. Jets screamed through the bitterly cold air like angry banshees, maintaining their protective envelope over the flotilla. At the edge of space, shadowy satellites turned on their axes and focused on the area as they were retasked from darkened rooms at CIA headquarters in Langley.

He nodded at his stone-faced exec as he took his post. His second in command gave him a look that said, 'All quiet.' He sat in the command chair and reached over for the mug of steaming coffee placed there prior to his arrival. As he lifted it to his lips the intercom crackled into life.

"Con, radio, we are receiving Flash Traffic. Emergency Action Message. Recommend Alert One, Recommend Alert One!"

The Captain, not quite believing what he had just heard, studiously replaced his untouched coffee and picked up the microphone next to him. "Con, aye. Alert One. Alert One. Set Action Stations. Alert One. Alert One."

He glanced at the exec again. His expression betrayed nothing. Neither did the captain's. Eighteen seconds later, the ship's weapons officer arrived breathlessly at the con with a flimsy sheet of paper. He caught his breath briefly and spoke, his voice only barely controlled.

"Captain, we have received a properly formatted Emergency Action Message from COMCINCPAC authorizing Strategic Missile Launch. Request permission to authenticate."

The captain nodded. His exec unlocked a panel next to him and took out a card encased in perspex. He broke it in two, removed the document inside, and checked the reference number against that on the paper brought to the bridge by the weapons officer. He looked at the Captain.

"Message is authentic. I concur, the Message is authentic."

The commander slowly reached for the microphone again. Pausing for a brief moment to ensure that he'd really heard what he'd heard, he spoke.

"This is the captain. Set condition one SQ for strategic missile launch. Spin up missiles six through ten and fifteen through nineteen. The release of nuclear weapons has been authorized. This is not a drill. Chief of the boat, all stop. Make your depth two hundred feet."

"All stop, depth two hundred feet, aye sir," responded the Chief.

The captain's mind raced. The carrier group wasn't yet in place and the last report he'd received said that the Chinese fleet was only just making preparations to sail. That was just hours ago. They couldn't have even put to sea yet. There couldn't have even been a confrontation, unless the

Chinese had initiated a pre-emptive missile strike against the Taiwan. That was unlikely. They certainly wouldn't have made a nuclear strike. Why destroy what they coveted so much? And yet his orders were for a nuclear strike against the Chinese mainland. His exec interrupted his thought process. "Target package sir," he said, thrusting a bound book into his hand marked 'Top Secret'. The captain scanned it briefly. The submarine pens at Jianggezhuang. The nuclear testing faculty at Mianyang, the naval base at Qingdao and, Jesus, Beijing. When he let his birds fly it was full blown nuclear war.

The intercom cracked into life again. "Con, missile control. Fuelling commenced. Ready to launch in eleven minutes by my mark." Picking up the microphone the captain replied slowly with a calmness he didn't feel. "Very well, keep me informed. Eleven minutes. Eleven minutes before he launched Armageddon. Whatever the Chinese had done, his launch would trigger an all out nuclear exchange. Either they had done something unthinkable, like pre-emptively nuking Washington, which made no sense whatsoever, or the hawks in the war room had a take he wasn't privy to. Not that it was his job to be in the picture totally, especially when time was in short supply. His job and course of action was well defined. He'd trained for it almost all of his life. Once given the authenticated command he was to fire his missiles, period. He had eleven minutes to ponder on it.

He was a patriot and a soldier. He was also highly intelligent. With only a moment's hesitation he then broke the first rule of his training and launch protocol. He glanced up at his exec, who was watching him intently. He nodded him over and under the pretence of studying the target package, he spoke quietly so no one else could hear in the noise of the con. "Speak totally freely number one. Speak off the record. Quietly." His exec looked around briefly and whispered. "This can't be right. Unless the Chinese have nuked the U.S. this just doesn't make sense."

"Agreed," replied the Captain. "This is my call number one. I'm going to try and get a confirmation. That on its own will end my career. Are you going to make this easy or hard for me?"

The exec hesitated for a moment. "You're the captain. To fire those missiles, both you and I have to concur. That's the rule. Unless we insert our launch keys simultaneously, the birds won't fire. If you say we fire, then I trust your judgment. I work for you. I concur that the message is genuine. I concur that we fire if you say so. If you want to check and I agree then my career is over too. So be it. My career is over. It's too important."

"Missiles fully fuelled in ten minutes." The weapons officers' metallic voice echoed around the con.

The captain looked up. "Chief of the boat, launch the communications buoy."

"Communications buoy, aye, sir."

The exec looked at the captain, "If we don't get confirmation…"

"I know," said the captain, "This is what we're here for."

"Communication buoy on station, Sir."

The captain picked up the microphone, "Sparks, get COMCINCPAC on the horn."

"Pardon Sir, please repeat," was the astonished reply.

"Just do it," snapped the Captain.

"Missiles fully fuelled in nine minutes."

"Con, radio. Can't raise COMCINCPAC. Just static out there."

The captain squeezed the microphone ever harder. "Try the fleet, there's half a million tons of U.S. Naval hardware up there." He glanced at his exec. "They've got to know something." As he spoke, he was aware he was way out of his jurisdiction. His exec moved closer.

"Not being able to raise COMCINCPAC doesn't mean it's been destroyed. The only way to get a clear signal is to break surface. If we do that and the shit really has hit the fan, we'd be compromising our position. We'd be a sitting duck. They'd be waiting for us to pop up."

"Con, radio. Can't raise the fleet."

"Missiles fully fuelled in eight minutes."

The blatant breaks in clearly defined nuclear launch protocol were causing odd looks from the con crew. The captain was aware of the nervous glances from sweaty, frightened young men.

"Sonar, range to fleet?" He needed to confirm the fleet was still in existence.

"Con, sonar. Fleet out of range, sir. Too far away for a clear sonar contact. I can read metal, and lots of it, but they're too distant to make out single vessels."

"Jesus," spat the exec. "It could just be wreckage he's reading or the fleet could still be there."

"Missiles fully fuelled in seven minutes."

The captain's mind raced. "Number one, how soon could we clarify the condition of the fleet if we chase them at flank speed?"

The Exec shook his head slowly. "Twenty eight minutes sir. There's not enough time."

"Number one, join me in the corridor please," he said, loudly enough for the con crew to hear. He ignored their astonished glances and strode off the bridge, closely followed by his exec.

"Bob. Our careers are fucked anyway but I'm being asked to destroy the planet with zero information. If the brass has called this wrong and we fire, then the Chinese will retaliate with everything they've got. If even half of their missiles get through our defences, then every major city in the U.S. will be wiped out. Once the Chinese missiles are in the air then our defence systems will pick them up and order a full ballistic retaliation and do the same to China. Half the world will be uninhabitable for centuries."

"You're assuming," replied the exec, "that the Chinese haven't made a pre emptive strike. If they have then we're part of that retaliation and Chinese missiles are already on their way to the States as we speak."

"But it doesn't make sense," argued the captain, "Why would they do that? They know there's no way to win. And they're out to get Taiwan. Attacking the mainland U.S. wouldn't help and nuking Taiwan wouldn't help. It's like using a sledgehammer to crack a nut, plus the fact that you couldn't even eat the nut when you'd cracked it."

"Missiles fully fuelled in six minutes."

"Nonetheless, Captain. This is what we're here for. This is what we do. This is our purpose."

"No, dammit," hissed the captain, "What we're here for is to actually prevent what we're about to do. We're a deterrent. We're too awful to contemplate."

"Evidently not," replied the exec. "Our bluff has been called. Whatever's happened up there, our bluff has most definitely been called."

"Something's missing, or we're missing something." The captain ran his hand through his hair. "We're not even supposed to be having this conversation and yet we are. We're having it because it feels wrong. Something's wrong,"

"Have you considered," his number one offered, "that this could never feel right? It would always feel wrong."

There was a long pause while the two men fought with their intellects, trying to rationalise the situation.

"Missiles fully fuelled in five minutes."

The captain straightened up, "I'm not going to push that button until I know it's right. We're going to make for the surface so we can get a clear signal."

"If we do that and it's really going down up there then we'd be an easy target."

"I know. My rationale is this. If a fully blown confrontation is going on, then our few missiles aren't going to make any difference either way.

There's no way to win a nuclear war. If we fire and the order is correct our firepower is still surplus to requirements. If we don't fire and the order is an error, then you and I will end up in the brig but millions will live."

"So you're betting that the Chinese haven't already attacked and that therefore we won't be blown out of the water the moment we surface. You're gambling. You're thinking that the best case scenario is that hostilities haven't started and you'll go to jail for not following orders. OK, it's a good gamble. But consider this, the message was correctly formatted. The codes are unbreakable. We know that. We know that we've definitely been ordered to fire by our lords and masters, who have a fuller picture than we do. Why would they have issued the order in the first place? And if we start to debate that, then none of this makes sense and we're just simply disobeying orders and reneging on our oath to defend our country."

Both men stared at each other intently.

"Missiles fully fuelled in four minutes."

The exec grimaced. "Fuck, let's check."

The mighty vessel broke through the surface in a hail of spray. Eighteen seconds later a Chinese Silkworm missile hit the conning tower at twice the speed of sound, blowing the *USS Louisiana* out of the water.

Some thirty miles to the south, the Chinese commander of the super secret stealth boat silently thanked the powers that be for its radar invisibility and the courage of his superiors. Their plan was so perfect. They had been correct in their gamble that the weak Americans wouldn't have the stomach for a fight. Having lost a submarine before hostilities even started would weaken their resolve. Opinion at home would immediately question why their young were being lost yet again a long way from home in a confrontation that they had no right to be involved in. Their free media would howl for redress. While their politicians were busy giving sound bytes to the press, trying to justify yet another ill advised foreign policy venture, Taiwan would slip quietly and uncontested into Chinese hands. Their gamble that the decadent warriors of the west would never launch their missiles was the greatest bluff he'd ever seen. How could the Americans be so arrogant to believe that their codes could never be broken? The Chinese knew that they'd never obey their false order to fire without confirmation.

The minute the captain of the submarine had hesitated, and embarked on the thought process that had led him to surface and expose his submarine, Taiwan had been forever lost to the West.

- The End -

ABOUT THE AUTHOR

Based in London and New York, Alexander Hammond is an inveterate writer and traveller. *Tales from the Edge of Forever* is his third book but his first published work of fiction under this name. His non fiction has also been syndicated in many international newspapers and publications but imaginative fantasy writing is his first love.

Alexander Hammond Facebook page:
www.facebook.com/ahammondwriter